"Good evening,
Doctorrr Chamberrrs."

Lauren nearly burst out laughing at his attempted Scottish accent. She mastered her face just in time, though, and demanded, "What kind of shenanigans are you up to, may I ask?"

Finn must have felt the quiver of delight in her hand, for he smiled into her eyes and plunged ahead with his Scotsman's burr. "Shenanigans, you say? Don't you trrrust me, Laurrrie?"

"Of course I don't trust you! You're up to some trick, I can see."

"Ah, neverrr fearrr, fairrr lassie. I've come to rrrescue you frrrom this deadly place."

"Deadly? Finn, I—"

Finn tipped his head close to hers and, with a wink, confided, "Deadly dull, I mean. Come along, fairrr lass. My horrrse is waiting."

He shot a furtive glance around the place, and without explanation began to drag her across the room...

Dear Reader:

Romance readers today have more choice among books than ever before. But with so many titles to choose from, deciding what to select becomes increasingly difficult.

At SECOND CHANCE AT LOVE we try to make that decision easy for you—by publishing romances of the highest quality every month. You can confidently buy any SECOND CHANCE AT LOVE romance and know it will provide you with solid romantic entertainment.

Sometimes you buy romances by authors whose work you've previously read and enjoyed—which makes a lot of sense. You're being sensible . . . and careful . . . to look for satisfaction where you've found it before.

But if you're *too* careful, you risk overlooking exceptional romances by writers whose names you don't immediately recognize. These first-time authors may be the stars of tomorrow, and you won't want to miss any of their books! At SECOND CHANCE AT LOVE, many writers who were once "new" are now the most popular contributors to the line. So trying a new writer at SECOND CHANCE AT LOVE isn't really a risk at all. Every book we publish must meet our rigorous standards—whether it's by a popular "regular" or a newcomer.

This month, and in months to come, we urge you to watch for these names—Jean Fauré, Betsy Osborne, Dana Daniels, Cinda Richards, and Jean Barrett. All are dazzling new writers, an elite few whose books are destined to become "keepers." We think you'll be delighted and excited by their first books with us!

Look, too, for romances by writers with whom you're already warmly familiar: Linda Barlow, Elissa Curry, Jan Mathews, Frances Davies, and Jasmine Craig, among many others.

Best wishes,

Ellen Edwards

Ellen Edwards, Senior Editor
SECOND CHANCE AT LOVE
The Berkley Publishing Group
200 Madison Avenue
New York, N.Y. 10016

Second Chance at Love®

DATING GAMES

ELISSA CURRY

**A SECOND CHANCE AT LOVE
BOOK**

Other books by *Elissa Curry*

Second Chance at Love
TRIAL BY DESIRE   #174
WINTER WILDFIRE   #178
LADY WITH A PAST   #193
BLACK LACE AND PEARLS   #213

To Have and to Hold
PLAYING FOR KEEPS   #18
KISS ME, CAIT   #23

With many thanks to Charlie Simmons at OSF Computers.

chapter 1

"WHY ARE WE stopping here?" Lauren Chambers questioned the driver of the downtown-Baltimore bus as he pulled in at the corner instead of at the regular bus stop in front of the building that housed her professional offices.

"That's why." Glowering, the bus driver gestured at the windshield, through which Lauren saw that the usual stop was blocked by an illegally parked bright red limousine with a District of Columbia license plate.

"Ah." Lauren's eyes widened slightly as she took in the long length of the gaudy limo.

"It's probably one of those Arab sheiks, right, lady?" the bus driver appealed to her. "Rich guys have no respect for the law."

"Maybe it's an eccentric millionaire," Lauren offered cheerfully as she stepped down to get off the bus. She turned to give the driver a smile. "Could be he's looking for someone to take a whole lot of money off his hands."

The driver pushed his cap back from his forehead and grinned. "Keep your eyes open for him, miss. Maybe you'll be the lucky lady."

Lauren laughed and got off the bus, briefcase in hand, savoring the bright sunlight of the May morning. In celebration of approaching summer, she had tied a jaunty pink ribbon in her hair and let the dark tresses hang in a loose pageboy instead of pinning them up in the usual sleek twist at the back of her head. Now, her hair blew against her throat, stirred by the salty breeze off the harbor just two blocks away. Lauren took a deep, cleansing breath and tipped her face up to the sun. With a good attitude and a little magic, this Monday might turn out to be painless after all.

Spirits high, Lauren breezed around a newspaper kiosk and nearly plunged straight into a sidewalk baseball game. It was a group of kids—three devilish-looking boys who were apparently skipping classes and a little girl in a parochial-school uniform. With them was a very tall man in a blue business suit, cowboy boots, string tie with an Indian-made clasp, and a gunslinger's Stetson hat. He looked out of place in staid Baltimore wearing that Western getup, and he seemed perfectly unaware of the fact that, along with the children, he had effectively stopped rush-hour traffic.

Several dozen commuters stood around watching the game with bemused, perhaps wistful, smiles. Spring fever was obviously rampant, Lauren reflected, pleased that she wasn't the only victim. With her own smile broadening at the scene, she skirted the outfield where morning pedestrians were watching the game as if it were a bit of street theater.

As she walked, Lauren watched the tall cowboy wind up for the pitch with a great, comical contortion of his long legs. A few yards away, the little girl crouched in a batter's stance, holding the plastic bat at the ready.

"Easy out!" yelled the boy at first base—the mailbox by the corner.

The cowboy let loose the pitch, and the crowd held its collective breath in anticipation. The Wiffle ball made a slow arc and the little girl wound up tight, waiting for the precise moment with her face screwed up in a mask of fierce concentration. Then she swung, connected beautifully, and the ball went flying.

The cowboy back-pedaled for the catch, yelling, "It's a high fly! Out of the ballpark! Look at it go!"

Instinct took over, and Lauren dropped her briefcase on the sidewalk and started forward. Laughing, she called, "I've got it, coach!"

The cowboy was almost upon her. Lauren stretched up, eye on the descending ball, and the cowboy spun around. Wham! They collided like two outfielders after the same catch. Wind blown out of her, Lauren gave a surprised, laughing cry and bobbled the ball. The cowboy's hands went around her waist to steady her, to keep her from falling, and the ball bounced harmlessly onto the sidewalk.

Lauren stared straight up into the man's eyes and felt the world freeze in the most idiotic, heart-stopping moment of her life.

The crowd cheered, and someone yelled, "It's a home run!"

Only dimly aware of the spectators, Lauren continued to gaze up at the man whose arms encircled her. He was handsome and laughing, his dark brown eyes full of mischief and delight. His smile was quick and a little crooked, his brows straight, his jaw long and square. From under his wide-brimmed hat, now cocked back on the crown of his head, showed very dark curly hair, a little longer than was fashionable. His eyes crinkled with fun at the corners, and his hands felt firm and confident sliding around her waist for a better hold. Lauren dropped her own hands instinctively to his chest, unconscious for a split second that their bodies were still locked together by the momentum of the collision.

"You'll never make the majors, Miss Mantle," the cowboy chided her. His voice was a light baritone, but rich with laughter.

"That's Ms. Mantle to you, coach," she retorted automatically.

His eyes widened, and his grin promptly collapsed into an expression of contrite surprise. He loosened his grip on her and said blankly, "Oh. Of course. I'm sorry."

Lauren laughed at his sudden transformation into a crestfallen little boy. "Goodness, I didn't mean—look here, it was just the first thing that came into my head."

"I'm sorry," he said again, and he let her go completely, stepping back a pace as if for safety. The apprehension so apparent in his face made Lauren think of an earnest youngster caught in some truly regretted act. Brown eyes brimming with doubt, he asked, "Did I hurt you?"

"Don't worry." Psychologist that she was, Lauren tried to put the stranger at ease with a friendly grin. "You just spared me the embarrassment of landing on my backside on the sidewalk!"

Tongue-tied, the man hastily bent to retrieve Lauren's fallen briefcase. Once below her, though, he couldn't seem to stop a quick and instinctive glance up the length of Lauren's shapely legs. Slim, feminine shoes, then pale, pretty stockings stretched over calves whose muscles were kept firm by occasional bicycling, and then the suggestion of curving thighs beneath a cleverly cut pastel plaid skirt. His automatic but appraising glance only seemed to increase the cowboy's confusion, and when he stood up again, he snatched off his hat and bashfully avoided Lauren's eyes. The logical retort slipped out anyway, as on a gulp he said in a soft and shy west-Texas drawl, "It would sure be a lucky sidewalk, ma'am."

"Compliment accepted, sir," Lauren said, laughing again as she took the proffered briefcase. Their hands met on the leather, his dry and warm under Lauren's. She didn't pull the briefcase away just yet, but met his dark brown eyes again and absorbed the liquid warmth of his gaze. The morning breeze ruffled his already tousled dark hair, making Lauren think of woolly puppies—big ones, of course, but cute nevertheless. A funny tug caught at her inside, a queer and puzzling inward twist.

The cowboy released the briefcase and smiled shyly once more. He cleared his throat but seemed unable to find the right words, then reached into his pocket. An instant later, he brought his hand out and flicked his wrist with a magician's flourish. He made a tunnel of his fingers, then puckered up and blew inside his palm and—presto! A paper daisy flipped magically into his fingers. He presented the flower to Lauren and bowed over it.

"Awww," sighed the crowd around them, touched by the romantic gesture.

Lauren blushed like a schoolgirl and accepted the flower from his hand. Their fingers met, brushed, and fell away rather slowly. "Thank you," Lauren murmured. She tipped the daisy to her nose—though it held no scent—to hide her smile from him. "You're very sweet."

The cowboy's gaze began to fill with pleasure once again, gradually losing the shadow of uncertainty. He said shyly, "No hard feelings then? You're not hurt?"

"Only my pride. Really, I'm fine. I'm sorry for—for sounding so mean," Lauren apologized gently. She sensed that she could devastate this charming but curious fellow with the wrong remark. "About the Ms. Mantle thing, I mean. It wasn't a reprimand, really, just a thoughtless retort."

"*I* was thoughtless," he corrected quietly, again with the endearing half-smile. "I make a lot of social blunders like that. Sorry."

It was his face, Lauren decided, that was so extraordinary. As she hesitated on the sidewalk, half-conscious that around them other people had begun to drift away to their own concerns, she watched his expression as the tall and lanky cowpoke struggled to find a socially acceptable speech for the occasion. He had an honest face, the kind that young children possess before they learn to master their thoughts and keep their feelings inside. His dark eyes and quick, sensitive mouth were open, transparent, totally revealing the man inside. An odd sensation stole over Lauren as she held his expressive eyes with her own, as though an image of the future had just flitted through her mind. It was a hazy image of a quiet, intimate evening by a fireside, or maybe of an open ocean seen from the misty microcosm of a sailboat deck.

Remembering the time and place, however, she brushed off the fleeting sensation. Her brain was going a little haywire today, probably because of the unexpected collision with a very attractive, rather intriguing masculine body on a warm spring morning. She decided to keep the paper flower. How often does a lady get a daisy from a cowboy magician—even if he could hardly put two words together without blushing? She should have kissed his cheek for the flower, she realized belatedly. He might have fainted with the shock, of course, but the crowd would have loved it. Lauren smiled. If this bashful cowboy could hear her subconscious talking, he'd really saddle up Old Paint and escape to the lone prairie! He smiled back at her, though, and Lauren had the odd feeling that he had indeed read her thoughts.

In the next instant, he was engulfed by the kids who had been playing ball. The little girl tugged at the cowboy's sleeve. "Didja see me, mister? I hit a homer! Can we do it some more?"

He hesitated, and Lauren felt the spell of intimacy between them break. He looked so much like a Great Dane puppy in the wrong litter just then that she nearly laughed. The little girl was insistently pulling his sleeve and there was no escape. He gave Lauren another quick smile, apologetically this time, and lifted his shoulders as if to say, "Duty calls."

She returned his smile ruefully and tried to come up with a parting line, a nice farewell. None came to mind, so she reached out impulsively and touched him once on the arm. Yes, he did exist, all right. But the kids were clamoring for recognition and she couldn't think what to say, so Lauren turned away without a word. Time to get back to the real world. Her first few steps were slow, but then she picked up speed. After all, chance encounters happen all the time, she reasoned. Why should she imagine this one was something special?

She went up the marble steps of her office building without a backward glance, though for some reason she was sure the tall cowboy was watching her. She resisted the impulse to turn and give him another look herself, and instead touched the flower he had given her to her cheek, as though to assure herself of the reality of the entire episode.

Odd how some little moments in life could seem so monumental sometimes. Shaking her head, Lauren pushed through the double doors and went straight toward the elevator bank.

There was an enormous poster propped on an easel beside the waiting elevator, and the sight of it blew all thought of the appealing cowboy completely out of Lauren's mind.

The offending poster was another advertisement for Interface, that silly computer dating service on the same floor as her office. It portrayed a leering man and an ecstatic woman frolicking on a pink beach, and the message scrawled in juicy letters below the picture gushed, "Love can find a way even in the computer age!"

With a wry face at the ridiculous poster, Lauren marched onto the elevator and punched the fifth-floor button. The real world of Monday morning had begun. No use trying to pretend otherwise. Her running feud with Interface was about to heat up again.

It had started eight months ago, when that cursed company had moved into the building in—of all places—the office directly across the hall from Lauren's own. Lauren was a marriage counselor, and jokes about her being located so close to the dating service began as soon as Interface set up shop.

To make matters even more uncomfortable, Interface, a nationally franchised organization, found Baltimore very fertile ground, indeed. Single people came in droves to join up. Interface was constantly expanding its office space to accommodate the increasing business. Other professionals like Lauren as well as companies that had originally been located on the fifth floor were asked to move—with financial compensation, of course—so that Interface could enlarge its facilities. Lauren was the last holdout. And she'd be darned if she was going to give in to the pressure and move! She disapproved of dating services for many reasons. Not least of which was that a number of her clients had originally met their spouses through such organizations. A computer might be able to predict a superficial attraction between two people, Lauren thought, but clearly it was no judge of what was necessary for a successful marriage.

Briefly, Lauren had wondered if some small remnant of bitterness over Josh Redmond's leaving for the bright lights of Wall Street had stimulated her animosity for a company that promised eternal romance, but she'd brushed the thought aside. She had learned a lot about herself when she and Josh broke up, and she considered herself mature and perceptive enough not to let her personal experiences impair her professional judgment.

Lauren sighed. At the least, she would have to face that sneaky, slippery, sometimes semihysterical Interface manager Musgrave again today. She wasn't looking forward to that confrontation, even though she had stood her ground against the man in all their prior encounters. Musgrave had threatened to call in the company president to deal with Lauren on the office-moving situation, and company presidents were undoubtedly tougher adversaries than the lower-echelon members of management. Moreover, this president, with the name of Finnegan T. Gallagher III, certainly sounded like an indomitable curmudgeon to Lauren.

The elevator opened its doors, and she stepped out and walked across the hallway to the door that read LAUREN E. CHAMBERS, PH.D., FAMILY COUNSELING. Time to get to work, she told herself as she put her hand on the doorknob.

Yet, here was the daisy, still in her fingers. Lauren twirled it once playfully, then again, thoughtfully. With one last wistful thought for spring baseball games with carefree cowboys and little children, Lauren pushed through her office door. She was smiling in spite of that cursed dating service.

chapter 2

THE OFFICE LIGHTS were on, the radio was already crooning softly, the plants had been watered, and the smell of coffee wafted pleasantly in the air. All's right with the world after all, Lauren thought with a grin.

Billy Jorgensen, Lauren's assistant, was at his desk blithely cranking a piece of stationery into the typewriter. He glanced up, and his quirky face curved into a pleased smile. "Good morning, Doctor Chambers!" he called.

Billy was slim and neat and sandy-haired. He was a perennial student in constant search of an elusive master's degree. He had graduated from college with a B.A. in English, but having minored in economics he had a brief but unsatisfactory flirtation with that subject at the graduate-school level before switching to sociology. Now he was financing his study of psychology by working as Lauren's assistant. Billy did not like the word "secretary" because of its demeaning connotations, but he performed all the functions of Lauren's previous secretarial help. His typing was slow but accurate. The accuracy was all that really mattered to Lauren, and Billy was almost neurotically precise in everything he did. He was also punctual, tidy, polite on the telephone, and he made a wonderful assortment of flavorful coffees.

Billy was a gem of an assistant, and in the last eighteen months he had evolved into a good friend and safe confidant for Lauren. She rather hoped that Billy wasn't going to get his act together to finish his graduate work too soon. She'd hate to lose the man she'd come to think of as an indispensable factotum and even a sort of younger brother.

"Hi," Lauren greeted him as she plunked her briefcase on the edge of his desk. The framed movie poster over Billy's workspace today was Errol Flynn swashbuckling in *Captain Blood*. Billy changed posters every few weeks, and this was a choice Lauren approved of wholeheartedly. With a smile for Errol, she twirled the flower in her fingers and asked, "Billy, do you believe in anything at first sight?"

"Anything?" Billy asked carefully, a grin starting around the corners of his mouth. "Like love, you mean?"

"Not necessarily. Anything. Curiosity, maybe. Or relief in knowing that nice people still exist in the world."

"Is this leading somewhere?" her assistant inquired patiently. During the last year and a half, Billy had come to know—if not understand—most of Lauren's moods. "Somewhere specific, that is? We can skip a lot of steps if you'd just tell me about the guy."

"What guy?"

"The guy who has you looking all dreamy-eyed this morning. You haven't broken a rule and slept with someone, have you?"

"No," Lauren said, firmly this time. There were many men in her life these days, but none to whom Lauren felt much attached. Not since Josh had there been a man Lauren thought she could make a long-term commitment to, and Billy knew it. She said, "Not even close. I just had my confidence in mankind renewed, that's all. It's kind of refreshing."

"You had a great weekend," Billy noted with doleful sarcasm. "I can tell."

Lauren placed the daisy on top of her briefcase. "It wasn't all that great, to tell the truth. But what's the news this morning?"

"I think you know already," Billy countered lightly, his hazel eyes dancing as he looked over the rims of his tortoise-shell glasses. He folded his hands in his lap and propped his Hush Puppies on a conveniently open desk drawer. Billy had gotten a haircut over the weekend, Lauren noticed—very, very short, as was his custom—and he had deigned to wear a tie today, a blue knit to match his plaid shirt. He said, "I read your article over the weekend."

"What article?" Lauren asked, reaching for the morning's mail and playing dumb.

"The innocent routine won't work with me—or with half the people who called this morning," Billy advised. "The *Baltimore* magazine article, of course. Where controversy goes, there goes Dr. Chambers. You outdid yourself this time, Lauren."

The article was a subject Lauren had hoped to avoid for at least another hour this morning. She flipped through the small stack of envelopes, glancing at the return addresses and pretending to be casual. "Did I? I thought the writing was rather good."

"Terrific, in fact. You're an even better writer than I thought, with a real flair for humor. The piece was great for laughs. I'm not sure Interface is going to be amused, though."

No, Lauren thought, Interface was definitely not going to be amused by her article. One of Lauren's many men friends, Jeremy Blythe, was an editor for *Baltimore* magazine, and he had laughingly listened to her frequent reports about her running battle with Interface. Jeremy had become interested in dating services as a whole and had asked Lauren, in her capacity as a family counselor, to write an article about computer-arranged matches. Lauren had enthusiastically accepted his invitation to write an unbiased but humorous piece.

The fact that dating services continued to be something Lauren disapproved of after all her research had nothing to do with her fight with Interface. That's what she'd told herself, anyway. A kernel of guilt was germinating in Lauren's head, however. She had written a funny, tasteful, but nevertheless satirical article, blasting her latest pet peeve. The story had hit the magazine racks of Baltimore over the weekend, and now it was time to face the fallout generated by her remarks.

"Believe me," Billy said as he reached for his note pad, "we've had lots of phone calls bright and early this morning."

"Interface?" Lauren guessed with a pained smile.

Billy laughed at her expression. "Bull's eye! And about a dozen other calls. One crank, as a matter of fact."

"A satisfied Interface customer threatening me with a loaded floppy disk?"

"They're not customers at Interface," Billy corrected lightly. "They're called members." He adjusted his glasses to read his notes aloud. "Our old pal Musgrave has called twice. Dr. Wilson phoned about a client. And . . ." Billy glanced up meaningfully. "Jeremy Blythe wants to talk with you."

"Ah," Lauren said quietly, and she let her breath out in an uneasy sigh. "Jeremy, huh? I suppose the editor gets as much flak as I do about the article."

Billy's look was long and measuring, and he did not move from his ultrarelaxed position below her. "I had a distinct impression that this was a more personal matter."

Lauren did not answer. She put the mail down very carefully. Among the men she'd been casually dating, Jeremy Blythe had most recently been the front-runner. But Lauren had no interest in expanding their relationship beyond the platonic stage. Jeremy had had other plans, though. Saturday night had been a carefully orchestrated play to get Lauren to take the next step. Her expression must have told Billy the outcome of the evening.

Billy blew a long-suffering sigh. "Lauren, you didn't walk out on another of his posh wingdings, did you? Saturday night?"

"Sorry." Lauren pulled an apologetic smile. "I couldn't

help it. You're not going to be disgusted with me, too, are you?"

"Blythe was?"

Lauren nodded. "Again. Honestly, Billy, it's just not my style. It was a bunch of his buddies from his old London magazine. The whole thing was very highbrow, very British—"

"Very stuffy."

Lauren nodded unwillingly. "Yes, I suppose you could say that. Not that I didn't enjoy myself for a while, mind you, but after hearing ad nauseum about their devil-may-care days of fifteen years ago, I just—"

"—couldn't stand it. You held out longer than I would have, I'm sure. Your tolerance for the intolerable has always amazed me." Bluntly, he asked, "Did Blythe lose his stiff upper lip with you yet? Take a cricket bat to your lovely little nose?"

Lauren sent a hard look down at her assistant, almost a glare that belied the fact that she was actually searching within herself for an answer to a deeper question. She looked away then and shook her head slowly, running her fingertips up the smooth leather of her briefcase. "No, he didn't. I deserve it, though. I'm not exactly sure why my heart doesn't go pitty-pat for Jeremy. There's nothing really wrong with him, you know."

"He's a man who needs a mother," Billy said decisively. He kicked his foot out of the drawer and sat up, spinning his swivel chair around until his compact body was positioned at the coffee maker. Plucking Lauren's cup from the small rack, he added, "He thinks he's found one in you. And you encourage him in that delusion, you know."

"Whew!" Lauren sighed dramatically, and she popped her eyes for a little comedy. "I'm glad that one of us understands how the human mind works!"

"I'm serious, Doctor," Billy responded calmly, ignoring the gentle nip of sarcasm in Lauren's words. "You pull that routine with a lot of men. I think it's your way of avoiding romantic involvement. You're strong and mature beyond your years, and you're very supportive. Those are qualities that are attractive, but you use them to keep men at arm's length."

"Give it to me straight, Billy. I can take it."

Billy passed her a steaming cup of coffee without batting an eye at her ironic tone. He said, "You're a good listener, Lauren. That's why you're successful at your work, I suppose. And it's probably why you're one of the most popular single women in Baltimore. But it doesn't excite you, does it, when men treat you like a shrink?"

"Or their mother?" Lauren asked rhetorically. She accepted the cup with an automatic "thank you," and blew across the rim. French vanilla in the coffee beans today, Billy's favorite. Lauren was silent, enjoying the pleasant fragrance of the hot liquid. Quietly, she agreed, "No, that's not my idea of excitement."

"Are you going to break things off with Jeremy?" Billy asked, driving directly to the point of the matter. He averted his face and refilled his own cup of coffee.

"I never started anything with Jeremy in the first place," Lauren said quickly. "Not really, that is. I've been dating other men right along. He knows that. If he wants to settle down in a house with a picket fence, though, I think he understands I won't be the little woman waiting in the kitchen every night for him to come home."

"I see," Billy murmured, glancing up. "So you already broke up with him."

"Yes," Lauren admitted with an explosive laugh that lacked any amusement. "And I suppose you've got a cure for me? Another one of your famous theories about my love life?"

"Who can argue with success?" Billy asked with a grin. "You've been having fun—the good, clean kind—for a couple of years. You've got the world by the tail, Doctor Chambers!"

"Maybe," Lauren said, and she drank deeply from her cup, scalding her mouth and not really caring. It felt good to bring that wave of heat up through her face until the tears glistened behind her eyes. No emotion stirred inside her, though Lauren knew she ought to be mourning yet another lost love. She had been emotionally devastated when Josh had departed for New York. He'd said he wanted to continue seeing her, but Lauren believed the truth of the wry maxim: "Absence makes the heart grow fonder—of somebody else." Sure enough, within a month Josh had met another woman in Manhattan, and his phone calls to Baltimore had gradually dwindled to nothing. Since that time there had been other men to say good-bye to. Each parting became easier, though, as if Lauren had been toughened up and could now step in and out of relationships unscathed. Today she felt curiously happy, oddly exhilarated. Jeremy was out of her life. She was relieved to be alone again.

There was the daisy on her briefcase. Lauren picked it up again.

"Okay, then," Billy said, cautiously watching her quick change of expressions. "I can see you don't need a pep talk, but bear with me for just one bit of advice."

"Are you giving me a choice?"

"No. What you need, Lauren, is no men at all for a while. Dating like crazy since your breakup with Redmond hasn't been very therapeutic, has it? Take a break from that frantic social schedule of yours. Turn down the first dozen men who ask you out this week—don't laugh! I'm the one who answers your phone, you know!"

"I don't get a dozen calls in one week!" Lauren objected with a smile.

"I'll start keeping track if you'd like me to prove my point," Billy said, and he reached for a pencil. He aimed it at her. "Just turn them down. When somebody new comes along with a strong ego and no need for a mother figure, then I give you permission to come out of hiding. Until then, you're grounded, Doctor!"

Lauren made a face at him. "You're getting too cocky, Mr. Jorgensen."

"Yes, but you're pleased that I've got the talent to run this operation of yours—and still have enough *chutzpah* to order you around. What would you do without me?"

"I don't want to think about that possibility," Lauren countered honestly, her smile one of genuine amusement.

"I've got enough on my mind this morning without worrying about replacing you."

Billy drew the leather-bound appointment book across the desk. "Well, let's see if I can't make things a little easier for you today. You seem to have a touch of spring fever. What can I do to help? Put your flower in water?"

Lauren smiled and brushed the daisy across her nose, caressing her skin with the delicate petals. She smiled. "No. I—hey, how about some baseball tickets, Billy? Would you like to go to a baseball game with me?"

Billy didn't seem surprised. "That's something we haven't tried yet. How could we have skipped baseball in our quest for the ultimate in Baltimore entertainment?"

"An unfortunate oversight," Lauren agreed with a grin. "What do you say?"

"Sure," Billy decided. "I'll call about tickets. Shall I round up the usual crowd of merrymakers and make a day of it?"

"Sounds good. Maybe Gloria will make one of her famous cheesecakes."

"You're supposed to have beer and hot dogs at the ball park," Billy corrected. "But if that's not your style . . ."

"Maybe you don't know all the sides of my style," Lauren said breezily, and she grabbed up her briefcase. Putting the daisy between her teeth, flamenco style, she picked up her coffee cup and headed for her office. Around the paper stem, she asked, "Anything important I ought to know about before the clients start coming?"

"Just one thing," Billy called after her, causing Lauren to turn in midstride. "It's Musgrave again."

Lauren made an about-face and set her coffee cup on the desk. She snatched the flower from her mouth. "Musgrave? He doesn't want to see me this morning, does he?"

"After that article you wrote about dating services?" Billy inquired. "Of course he wants to talk with you. But he called to say that the owner of Interface—the head honcho, the computer genius who actually owns all the Interface franchises all over the country—is on his way here from Washington to inspect their premises and okay their expansion project. Musgrave hinted that their almighty Mr. Finnegan T. Gallagher the Third would appreciate an audience with you to straighten out a few minor details."

"Finnegan T. Gallagher!" Lauren repeated, her laugh ringing suddenly. "I love that name!"

"The Third," Billy added, and he put his nose in the air in an imitation of what a Finnegan T. Gallagher III must look like. Very sophisticated, aloof, and well bred. He pursed his lips just so. "Musgrave said only that Gallagher wants a powwow with you about moving off this floor. But I feel certain that the subject of your article for *Baltimore* will come up as well."

Lauren grinned at Billy's act, teasing him. "And what did my stern taskmaster and illustrious assistant tell Musgrave?"

"That Mondays are your busiest days," Billy replied promptly. "That you have appointments with clients who have real problems, and that I doubted if you would even have time for lunch today, so he had better tell Finnegan T. to pick up his computer chips and go home."

Lauren cast a doubting glance at Billy. "Really?"

"Well," Billy corrected with a slow smile growing, "I think I was a little more diplomatic."

"Thank you," Lauren said. "Always be diplomatic, Billy, but don't give an inch."

"Right, exalted one." Billy took a noisy slurp of coffee. "So you want to duck Musgrave and the Gallagher character? I should hold the fort and repel all boarders?" He raised his free hand as if flourishing a sword, imitating the scene in the poster behind him.

"Something like that, Captain," Lauren agreed with another laugh at his mixture of metaphors and comedic attitude. "Just keep the authorized clients coming, Billy."

She pushed through the panel door to the larger, plusher office within. This was her lair, her own quiet spot where she could gather strength for the day or wind down on a Friday evening after a long week.

The off-white carpet—the color like the sandy beaches Lauren loved so well—was thick and silencing. The bookshelves were neatly lined with suitable texts but also scattered with little mementos—a perfect sand dollar, the bottle Lauren's dad had found on their scuba-diving ventures at the Canadian lake, the photo of her whole family crammed into a rowboat, for crabbing, with empty buckets raised in salute to Uncle Paul behind the camera.

Then there was a toy nutcracker, the colorfully painted kind of glowering soldier so readily found in department stores at Christmastime. Lauren's youngest brother, Jake, had sent it as a joke—a nutcracker for the nut-cracking psychologist. Jake was still working on an oil rig somewhere in the Gulf, playing practical jokes on his buddies, she supposed. A large Boston fern, a gift from her mother to commemorate the first anniversary of Lauren's professional practice, commanded the table by the window, looking regal and profuse as a result of Lauren and Billy's combined coddling.

The office was restful, familiar with the little objects that meant so much to Lauren and oddly separate from the rest of the world.

Lauren set her cup and the flower on the clean expanse of her sleek Danish desk and placed the briefcase carefully on the blotter. She unsnapped the catches and flipped the case open. Ah, the distinctive yellow bag. Lauren lifted out the bag of M&M's and proceeded with her Monday-morning ritual of restocking her stash of chocolates. A few of the candies went into the crystal egg on the corner of her desk, for her clients to help themselves to. The rest went into the pencil tray of her desk for surreptitious snacks during the week. Lauren popped two M&M's into her mouth, and, crunching the satisfying peanut centers with a grin, she walked around to the window. The spring sunshine was still bright and beckoning, and she pulled the cord to open the curtains. The harbor winked beyond the next building, and a scattering of gulls wheeled gracefully above the water.

Standing in the warm glow of the sun, Lauren blinked her eyes and closed them, thinking as the last of the chocolate melted sweetly down her throat that maybe Billy was right. Lately, she had to admit to feeling a bit out of sorts, a little empty perhaps, in spite of the friends—many of them men—who surrounded her.

Perhaps the busy social scene was why Lauren had taken on the cause of sticking with her old office in the face of the expanding computer dating service. But maybe she'd had enough polite cocktail-party chitchat and foreign films with subtitles. An old-fashioned knock-down, drag-out fight was sometimes good for the spirit. Three months ago, the Interface manager had come to Lauren, asking her to give up her lease on the fifth-floor office to make room for Interface's expansion. All the other leaseholders had agreed amicably, why couldn't Doctor Chambers? Musgrave had rubbed her the wrong way, and she'd been an unmovable rock in spite of his wheedling and threats. And now here she was fighting a battle with Finnegan T. Gallagher III's silly company!

Lauren didn't really have a squabble with the dating service in the beginning. Live and let live was usually her motto. But that little sneak Musgrave had chosen to pull a few fast tricks to get Lauren ousted from her office—tactics to get her discredited with the landlord. That was a different story. Now she was determined to stay. Let Gallagher and his merry band of matchmakers find a new place to plug in their computers.

Lauren peeped over the windowsill at the street below, searching for the long red limousine and the unlikely base-ball game on the sidewalk. What she wouldn't give to chuck her troubles and go for a walk! Maybe a vacation was in order. Lauren found herself smiling again, and she wondered what magicians from Texas did for relaxation. Just who was that adorable cowboy with the sensitive face?

But then Billy was buzzing through the intercom and the day's appointments began. Lauren sat composedly at her desk and fished two more chocolate candies out of the drawer for another quick fix. She put on her doctor's calm office manner before she pressed a slim finger to her own intercom and signaled for the first clients. Before the door opened, she whisked the paper flower off her desk and into the partially opened drawer. There, she could take a peek at it whenever she chose and not have to explain why a smile tugged at her lips each time.

Mondays were particularly busy for marriage counselors. Couples generally spent weekends together, and Lauren knew Saturdays and Sundays were prime times for marital troubles to erupt. She resigned herself to the usual Monday hulla-baloo. In fact, she enjoyed the tensions and complications. It gave Lauren satisfaction to help people find their way through the limitless labyrinths of human relationships.

Between two late-morning sessions, Billy stepped into Lauren's office for a quick message.

"You had a gentleman caller, Doctor Chambers," he announced. "A very importunate man. I didn't think he'd be so young, though."

Lauren looked up from her dictating. "Young? Who?"

Billy struck a pose, nose high. "Finnegan T. Gallagher the Third, of course. He's barely thirty, if he's a day. I figured he'd be a bald-headed professor type with a slide rule. He left this."

Lauren accepted the plain white business card. "He really stopped in?"

"Yes, indeed," Billy said, lifting the top of the crystal egg to steal a handful of chocolate candies. He added, "He was dressed as though he was headed for the Lone Star Cotillion. A cute sort of feller."

It couldn't be, Lauren thought with a smile growing on her face. Could it? Finnegan T. Gallagher III, owner of Interface, the baseball-playing cowboy from this morning? Lauren stared at her assistant for a moment, not seeing him. Finally, she focused her eyes and asked, "What did he say?"

"Just that he hoped you'd have time to see him while he was in town." Billy popped his M&M's one by one into his mouth and, around the mouthful, said, "I put him off."

"Thanks, Billy," Lauren murmured distractedly. She turned the card over in her fingers as Billy let himself out. The card was simple and straightforward. "Finnegan T. Gallagher"—no numeral after his name, but two Wash-ington, D.C., telephone numbers and what was probably a telex number, too, as well as a Georgetown address. He had not written any message on the card.

Lauren tapped the small cardboard rectangle on her desk. Somebody was in for a surprise, that was certain. Perhaps a meeting with the owner of that obnoxious dating-game scam might be worth the time. Lauren slipped the card into her skirt pocket with a smile. Time would tell.

She thought she would be prepared when it came to meeting Finnegan Gallagher, but as it happened, Lauren was almost scared out of her skin. It was after five o'clock, and Billy had gone home for the night. Lauren was just slipping out for a quick sandwich, and the doorknob stuck oddly in her hand. She yanked, and the office door flew open, released from the outside.

In the doorway stood her cowboy. Who was presumably Finnegan T. Gallagher III.

Lauren grabbed her throat to keep from crying out in surprise.

"You!" he exclaimed, recognizing Lauren immediately, clearly astonished at discovering her here. He had his Stetson hat in his hands, and his dark hair was just as tousled as before. His brown eyes were direct and wide with surprise. "You're not Dr. Chambers!" Lauren noted that this time he spoke with no trace of a Texas accent.

She gasped for breath, struggling for control. Rarely was anyone in the building so late in the afternoon, and she was still frightened. As her heart quit hammering, Lauren managed to say, "Y-yes. Mr. Gallagher, I take it?"

He didn't stay stunned for long, and he collected himself admirably. "I scared you. I'm sorry. I was just about to come in and speak to your—your—the guy who works in there."

"And I was just on my way out. No harm done."

His bashful grin was slow. The corners of his nearly black eyes crinkled, and there was a twinkle of pleasure in his gaze. When he spoke again, that languid Western drawl of his was back again. "Yes, ma'am. Mind if I come in and have a quick look around?"

"I don't mind, Mr. Gallagher," Lauren replied, and she stepped hastily out of his way. He hadn't seemed so tall before, and she flattened her body against the door. She added, "But I have a group-therapy session to conduct in an hour, and I—"

"I'll be finished before then," Gallagher said, and he took two long strides into the office. He looked around, gauging the quality of the place, it seemed, darting a look through the open doorway to Lauren's inner office. He even poked his nose through the conference-room door, and a moment later he came back, shaking his head with amusement. "This is what has little Musgrave so riled up? Not much room here to cause such a fuss."

"It's humble, but it's home," Lauren said, her voice containing a flicker of tartness along with some amusement. She waited by the door during his quick inspection, holding it open expectantly.

Gallagher turned and fixed a steady gaze on her. Without argument, without shyness for once, he said, "You mean to stay here."

"Yes," Lauren stated with quiet but equal firmness.

"Determined?"

"Absolutely."

"Okay," he said lightly, strolling to the window.

"Okay?" Lauren repeated, wary that he was giving up the fight so easily.

Gallagher enjoyed her expression, and he smiled. "Sure. It's not the office space that's got me interested in you. I'm sorry to say that it's not even your baseball skills, Dr. Lauren Chambers."

"Oh?" Lauren asked, calmly this time.

"Yes." Gallagher put his shoulder to the doorjamb of Lauren's inner office, and they faced each other across the small expanse of the outer room. He watched her with that same intent gaze that appraised and lingered. He explained abruptly, "I figure the time will come when you're just as uncomfortable sitting across the hall from my people as they are sitting across from you right now. What's got me up here today, Doctor, is what you've been sayin' about my little business over there."

"I see," Lauren said smoothly, fighting down a moment's nervousness. A showdown, was it? She wasn't sure she had her pistols loaded yet.

He noted her careful tone. "Don't go all chilly, Doctor," he coaxed. "I'd like to proposition you."

Something in the way he said the word brought Lauren up short. She stared into his black eyes, searching for a clue. Had he meant—? No, of course not. He wasn't the type to make such a calculated double entendre. Was he? No, the bashful look was back, and he smiled. If he was a lady-killer, he was the kind that relied purely on the woman's instincts.

Gallagher pushed off the doorway and came sauntering across the office again, a purposeful air about him now. "Come along," he commanded gently. "You were on your way out for some supper, I'll bet. My car's outside."

"Mr. Gallagher—"

"Come along," he repeated, taking her with a light grip under her elbow that defied disobedience. He steered her out through the door and into the hall.

Too late, Lauren hung back. Gallagher's shy-boy act was deceiving. Here he was dragging her out into the hallway with the suave determination of a man who'd seen every James Bond movie six times. Maybe his bashfulness was as fake as his Texas accent! Lauren faltered and belatedly tried to pull away. "Mr. Gallagher, I've got a therapy group coming in less than an hour!"

"No problem," he said, pulling her with him to the elevator. "We'll be back in plenty of time. I hear you do marriage counseling."

"Yes," Lauren said breathlessly, resisting his unbreakable grasp out of instinct. She tossed up her head to glare meaningfully at him, and demanded, "Are you interested?"

"Why, no, Doctor," Gallagher replied, his appreciative smile growing. His eyes were glimmering with amusement and sharpening interest as he added, "I'm not married."

chapter 3

THERE WAS NO time to be surprised. Once outside, Gallagher steered Lauren down the marble steps to the red limousine. The driver was a long-haired young man in jeans, wearing a cassette recorder on his belt and a set of headphones over his ears. He greeted Gallagher with a familiar and insubordinate, "Hi," then popped open the car door for Lauren.

"Long day, Steve?" Gallagher inquired, already yanking his string tie loose.

"Not bad," the young man responded as he tugged the headphones down to wear necklace style around the collar of his sweat shirt. He gave Lauren an impertinent up-and-down look and said with a leering grin, "The girls in this town are nice to watch."

Before she could retort, Gallagher gently prodded her into the plush and roomy back seat of the long car. Startled, Lauren began to climb over an amazing clutter of odds and ends to make room for Gallagher. A pair of running shoes, the Wiffle ball and plastic bat, a Spanish dictionary, half a dozen cassette tapes. The back seat was nearly obliterated by the rubble.

Lauren almost sat on a pocket-sized computer that lay half in and half out of an empty doughnut box. She picked it up, juggling the computer in one hand to brush the worst of some spilled popcorn off the seat and onto the floor. She shoved the shoes and a hat and the tapes into one consolidated pile and tried to think. There was a lot of information to assimilate. The man had manipulated her into a quick dinner date with the speed of a con artist, and now it looked as if he had maneuvered her into a car that doubled as his home away from home. Maybe he wasn't as harmless as he looked.

Gallagher laughed with the driver, then tossed his suit jacket into the car. A moment later, he climbed into the back seat with Lauren.

"How about a drink?" he asked, dropping his tie into his Stetson and dumping them both unceremoniously on the ledge behind the seat. The condition of the car's interior was apparently no surprise to him, and in fact he seemed to enjoy being tucked comfortably among his odd collection of goodies. He said without a trace of his earlier accent, "If you've got a long evening ahead, I recommend something with lots of sugar and caffeine."

In the space in front of the seat there was a mobile telephone, a television screen, and a paneled box. As Gallagher leaned over to open the box, Lauren realized that it doubled as a portable bar and a small refrigerator. A can of orange soda rolled out onto the floor, and Gallagher picked it up before it disappeared into the clutter of newspapers at their feet. "Orange?" he asked, deftly flipping the can end over end in one hand. "Or cola?"

Mystified by this strange creature who seemed to have arrived in conservative Baltimore from another planet, Lauren found herself smiling. She decided to go with the flow and said, "Cola, please. That can's liable to go off like Old Faithful when you open it."

"True, true. The cola's a better choice anyway, if it's extra energy you want," Gallagher replied, and he handed her an aluminum can without a flicker of uncertainty. It only took him a moment to get comfortable. He started to take the cuff links out of his shirtsleeves, evidently unaware that one link was an onyx stud and the other was gold with an engraved initial. He dropped one cuff link into his trouser pocket, but the other slipped through his fingers and went down through the seat. He didn't notice or didn't care, and said, "Cola is better than adrenaline, if you ask me. I wish I owned the patent. We'll have something light to eat in a couple of minutes, so you might as well—what's the matter?"

"Nothing," Lauren said, trying to match his aplomb with her own brand of poise. She glanced meaningfully at his discarded jacket, her brows high and her lips threatening to break into a grin at any moment. "I'm just wondering how far you're planning to undress, that's all. We've only just met, Mr. Gallagher."

Gallagher laughed and finished rolling his shirtsleeves up to his elbows. "Are you one of those old-fashioned girls, Dr. Chambers?"

"Yes. But in this town we're called women."

Gallagher froze—just for a split second and almost imperceptibly—and then he rushed to say with all politeness, "Of course. I'm sorry. I've done it again, haven't I?" Once again, he seemed genuinely regretful and a little shaken at having been caught in a sexist *faux pas*. His smile was apologetic and winning at the same time. "Forgive my manners. We computer types rarely come out into the real world, you know. My social skills are rusty."

"So I noticed," Lauren said lightly, wondering if his sudden innocence was an act. He had certainly dropped the cowboy routine as soon as the costume came off. What kind of an eccentric was he? She snapped the top off her can and automatically held the soda away from her pretty skirt.

The car eased forward and merged into the traffic. Gallagher relaxed into his side of the seat, stretching his long legs before him to get comfortable. Without his hat and cowboy tie, he looked almost like a normal businessman to Lauren's observing eye. He was very good-looking, she decided, and maybe a bit younger than she had first pegged him. No older than thirty, surely. His head was slim and narrow with that crown of too-long and unruly dark hair, and his face was quick to express what he was thinking. He looked as smart as the whiz kid he probably was, and full of vinegar, too. The sharp and slightly disconcerting glimmer in his eyes made Lauren keep her distance and her first impressions to herself a bit longer.

Gallagher popped open his own drink with unaffected pleasure. He lifted the can to her. "Cheers, Doctor."

Lauren took a short sip, watching him as he drank deeply. There was an appealing boyishness about Finnegan T. Gallagher, but Lauren did not want to make a mistake and take him too lightly. Keeping her voice neutral, she said, "You mentioned something about a proposition, Mr. Gallagher."

"So I did," he agreed, taking another pull of his drink while he sized her up again, more completely this time.

Lauren held still, silently wondering what he saw. Was he looking at the doctor? The diploma, the fancy office, and the expensive suit? Or did he see beyond that? The vulnerable woman in the guise of cool professional? She controlled the automatic urge to smooth her hair, but Gallagher must have divined her impulse, for his smile returned.

Emboldened by his unspoken approval, Lauren took the plunge without preamble. "If you're not concerned with my disinclination to move my office, Mr. Gallagher, you must be upset about the magazine article I wrote about dating services."

He smiled and said obliquely, "Free speech is one of our greatest rights. You had something to say, and somebody printed it."

"But you're bound to disagree with what I said," she asserted.

"That computer dating is degrading to women? That Interface and other dating services encourage sexually gratifying but short-term relationships that are emotional junk food?" Gallagher didn't appear to be the least bit angry. Just amused, maybe even taunting. He added, "I remember those phrases, among others you used. You have a way with words, Doctor."

"I'm a marriage counselor, Mr. Gallagher. I see what happens to people when they jump blindly into liaisons that—"

"Of course you do," Gallagher intervened smoothly. "Your article was based on your experiences as a counselor. And you probably had some valuable things to tell people. But I wonder if you did much research, Doctor."

"What do you mean?" Lauren demanded defensively.

"Have you ever used a computer dating company?"

"I thought you called it a personal introduction service," she shot back, bristling for a fight already.

He smiled broadly, as if seeking to put her at ease. "You've been talking to that character Musgrave. I've learned not to take him too seriously. Call a spade a spade, Doctor."

"Okay," Lauren said evenly. "No, I haven't made use of a computer dating service. I find other ways to make friends."

"Men friends?"

"Yes," Lauren said steadily. Remembering her psychologist's training, she stayed calm and explained without embellishment, "I have a generous circle of friends, both male and female."

"You're not married."

She instinctively touched her left hand with her right. He must have noticed she wasn't wearing any rings. "No, I'm not. But I do date, Mr. Gallagher. And I'm quite satisfied with my social life."

"Busy?" he inquired, lifting the soda can to his mouth once more. "Lots of men mooning around your doorstep?"

"Enough, thanks," Lauren said, unable to keep a smile at bay. He was direct and uncomplicated, and it was refreshing to find those qualities in a man. He had her off balance, steering her away from her practiced, psychologist's cool. It wasn't such a bad feeling, Lauren admitted to herself.

"I'm not surprised that you're popular," Gallagher observed, meeting her smile with another of his own. He didn't move, but stayed still as a cat and passed a very slow and suddenly very masculine glance down Lauren's figure. "You're an awfully attractive lady."

"You expected an old biddy, I'll bet."

He laughed and shrugged and fell into his joshing Texas drawl again. "My mistake, ma'am. I make a few. You're pretty as well as bright, Doctor, and you don't play those silly girl-boy games with your eyelashes. I'm glad to hear you've got a healthy, meat-and-potatoes sex life."

Lauren opened her mouth to object to his choice of words, but she realized at that moment that Finnegan T. Gallagher was very smart indeed if he was using this line of questioning to find out about her personal life. And that crazy accent was definitely a put-on, a fake that he used for some reason unapparent to Lauren. Following his lead, she chose to keep him guessing, and said mildly, "I'm glad you approve. Now, if—"

But the car had pulled to a stop, and when Gallagher realized where they were, he sat forward and tapped on the glass with his can. "The usual, Stevie-boy, but double the order this time."

They were in the parking lot of a fast-food restaurant.

At first Lauren thought they were having car trouble, but then she saw that their driver had rolled down his window of the limousine and was speaking into a microphone at the drive-up window. A family of three skipping children and a harried set of parents came out of the glass doors, paper bags of hamburgers in hand. The kids were fighting over possession of the milkshakes, and the parents turned and gaped at the idling luxury car with frank disbelief.

Lauren looked around at Gallagher in amazement. "You're kidding."

"About your social life?" Gallagher asked blithely and seemingly completely unaware that anything unusual was taking place. "No, I think it's good that our nation's troubled marriages are being tended by psychologists who have a firm grasp on their own personal lives. What concerns me, Doctor, is that you haven't really experienced the latest method of getting acquainted with other people."

Lauren wagged her head, a laugh beginning in her throat. This man was a character! She said, "All right, Mr. Gallagher, what's this leading up to?"

"Let's eat first," Gallagher suggested, and he sat forward again in the seat to receive the paper bags that Steve was passing through the glass partition. "I'm starving. Is there a park or something near here?"

"I—yes, just two miles or so, straight out this highway. Listen, Mr. Gallagher—"

"Hear that, Steve? Two miles up the pike." Gallagher closed the partition, then said to Lauren, "Look for the catsup, will you? I'm addicted to the stuff."

Lauren gave up with an amused sigh and put her nose into a large bag full of french-fried potatoes in little orange cardboard containers. There was bound to be catsup under all those fries, so she stuck her hand into the bag and groped around. She asked, "Are you leading up to what I think you're leading up to?"

A bargain?" Gallagher asked, and he lifted three Styrofoam hamburger packages out into the light. "Yep."

"Here's the catsup. What kind of bargain?"

"You've guessed it. I think you owe it to me to give Interface a trial, don't you?"

"A trial? You mean you seriously want me to join your company's computer dating service?"

"Of course." He traded bags with her and found a package of French fries to his liking. "Free of charge, naturally. In the interests of science, I'll give you a six-month membership in Interface, and you—"

"Six months!"

He stuck a french fry in his teeth like a cigar and looked at her, blinking innocently. "More? If you think six months is insufficient, I'll—"

"Not insufficient, no, just—"

"Have a hamburger. We order them without pickles, but if you'd like some, Steve can run around again and—"

"No pickles for me, thank you." Lauren looked helplessly at the meal that was beginning to spread out between them on the seat. She rescued a leaking packet of mustard before it stained the upholstery. Gallagher had hit her where it hurt—right in the guilt complex. Lauren's "unbiased" article hadn't been totally fair, and she was uncomfortably aware of that fact. In silence, she began a mental squirm.

"It's a straightforward proposal," Gallagher said, and he swallowed his first bite of hamburger with the gusto of a hungry teenager. "You enroll at Interface and go through the whole routine: the interview, the parties, dates, if you meet any men you want to see more of, and after six months you write another article."

"Who's going to publish it?"

He waved dismissively. "Let me worry about that. I'll buy an advertisement somewhere if I have to. I think the article's going to be interesting to some publisher, though. With a new perspective and the way you write, it's bound to be entertaining. It might make a good book, but that's probably thinking too big for now. What do you say?"

Lauren had been staring at the hamburger in her hands, and she had just worked up the courage to take a bite. With her mouth full, she shook her head in amusement. "You have a habit of thinking big, don't you?"

He smiled shyly again and propped his boots on the refrigerator. "People tell me that I do."

"You ought to start believing them." Lauren fished for some french fries and asked, "What's in this for me, Mr. Gallagher?"

"Besides the free opportunity to meet the man of your dreams through my company?"

Her look was wry, but amused. "Searching for the man of my dreams isn't the biggest goal in my life at the moment. I really have plenty of friends, Mr. Gallagher. I don't need any more."

"You never have enough friends," he countered, teasing. "Didn't your mother ever tell you that?"

"My mother taught Sunday school, and we got plenty of those lessons at home." The french fries were surprisingly good, and Lauren imitated his technique and took three in her fingers this time. "And under most circumstances I listen carefully to those old truisms. But this . . ."

"It's perfectly safe."

"And you'll pay my medical bills if Mr. Right turns out to be a crazy ax murderer?"

He laughed. "The possibility is so remote that I don't even have an insurance policy to cover that stuff. An ax murderer is not likely to be able to afford the fees we charge."

"Very comforting," Lauren remarked dryly, sending him a deadpan look.

"You need some inducement," Gallagher decided.

The limousine had traveled another couple of miles beyond the fast-food restaurant, and Steve found the entrance to the neighborhood park. He pulled the big car under some trees near the ball field and shut off the engine. After Steve had climbed out to eat his supper, which he spread out on the hood of the car, Gallagher opened another can of soda and said, "We'll make this fair, all right? If you write a second article after participating in Interface for six months, you may keep your office where it is now."

"Keep it?" Lauren echoed, laughing. "Thanks very much, Mr. Gallagher, but how can I receive what I already have?"

"Take it easy," he soothed her. "I'm talking about the whole floor of the building. If you do as I ask, Interface will move off the fifth floor and I'll continue to pay the rent—for two years, all right? You can have the whole darn floor to yourself and use it for whatever you like."

"What could I possibly do with all that space?" she demanded, amazed that he would come up with such a preposterous suggestion.

Gallagher shrugged. "I don't know. Aren't you bleeding-heart liberals always looking for places to do socially responsible things for the good of the less fortunate? Open a crisis hot-line headquarters. Give some space to runaway teenagers. A home for wayward kittens or something. I'll pay the bill."

"And get a nice tax write-off in the process?" Lauren asked with another laugh. He was harmless and bright and rather fun to spar with. She asked shrewdly, "Is that what you cold-hearted capitalists call charity?"

"I like arguing with you!" Gallagher declared with enthusiasm. He sat up straighter and grinned. "You think and talk the way I do!"

"I'm also not fooled by your overwhelming generosity," Lauren shot back. She put her tongue in her cheek and marshaled her smile. "What happens if I refuse your offer?"

"Refuse? Don't even consider it," Gallagher pleaded, his dark eyes full of mischief.

"Is there a threat coming?"

He chuckled. "Okay, here it is. If you don't write that article for me, Doctor—"

"You and your flunkey Musgrave are going to make my life miserable, right?"

"Did I say that?"

"You were going to."

"I would never threaten a lady."

"I'm no lady, I'm a psychologist."

He smiled ingenuously again and passed her another bag. "Have a milkshake, Doctor."

Lauren finished her hamburger and accepted the milkshake, touching Gallagher's hand inadvertently as she did so. Electrically, her eyes lifted to his, finding Finnegan T. Gallagher watching her expression with undisguised curiosity.

Until that moment, Lauren had been intellectually aware that they were a man and a woman alone in a car, but as if someone had flipped on a light in her head, she suddenly felt the full impact of the situation. Gallagher was an attractive man—oddly, he was more attractive than he seemed to realize. Somewhere in the depths of her own psyche, Lauren felt the stirrings of an ancient and somewhat disquieting response. Something very exciting existed in the air between them, and suddenly Lauren felt absurdly pleased.

When the silence became too full of static, Lauren collected herself again and asked directly, "Do you use Interface yourself, Mr. Gallagher? Are you enrolled in your own company's program?"

"Me?" he inquired nonchalantly. He leaned toward her again and stuck a straw into the milkshake she held in her hands. He stayed close for another instant, perhaps enjoying the proximity as much as Lauren was. He said in a low, confidential voice, "To tell you the truth, no, I'm not."

"You have plenty of women mooning around your doorstep already, is that it?"

"I have enough," he answered carefully. He sat back again and his eyes were steady, his slight smile in place. "I'm not a womanizer, to be honest. I know that's supposed to be the image of the young tycoon who's got more money than he can spend on cocaine, but I lead a very quiet life. Squiring scads of women all over the world doesn't interest me much, believe it or not."

"Good grief. You spend your days holed up with a computer that you call Delilah or something, right?"

"My work keeps me very busy," he admitted, going cagey.

"Interface is *that* interesting?"

He laughed at her tone. "You make it sound worse than it is. Interface is interesting, from a computer point of view, at least. I'm always tinkering with the program. But . . ."

"Yes?"

"Interface isn't my only business. I have—there are lots of irons in the fire."

"Goodness," Lauren sighed, sipping her chocolate shake. "I've never met a real tycoon before."

"Wh-what a thrill, right?"

She couldn't be sure, but Lauren suddenly sensed that Gallagher was on the verge of blushing. She watched his eyes, but he looked away and reached for the electric window button. He rolled down the window at his back and let the cool evening air drift into the car. So! In addition to being as lanky and plainspoken as a young Jimmy Stewart, he was as modest and as humble—even down to the halting smile and occasional stammer.

His profile was silhouetted against the open window, and watching him, Lauren asked abruptly, "How old are you?"

He laughed, surprised. "A tycoon has to be at least sixty-five, right?"

"No, I-I—" Lauren found herself stuttering, something that almost never happened to her. It must be contagious.

"I don't know why I asked, truthfully. I just—I wondered, that's all."

"Thirty-one. Surprised?"

"No, not really," Lauren said bluntly. "That is, you don't look any older. But it's a very young age to have achieved so much. I'm just thirty-one myself."

"Really? You seem older."

"Thanks," she replied tartly, annoyance showing at his inadvertent insult. "You're a charmer, aren't you?"

"I didn't mean that you actually *look* older, you just try to *act* older, don't you?"

Lauren made an exasperated face. "This is the second time today that somebody has tried to outshrink the shrink."

"I'm sorry," he said, going contrite like a little boy once more. There it was again: that immediate sensitivity that opened his face and brought a painful pang to Lauren's stomach.

"No need for apologies," she said quickly, gently.

"I was right then."

Lauren faced him, surprise flitting across her face as she realized he was serious. "That I try to act older? Why should I do that?"

He shrugged, amused. "You're the psychologist, I'm not. Why indeed, Doctor? Do you have to be a sixty-five-year-old shrink before anyone takes you seriously? All those pictures of Freud—"

"I don't have to be any older to do my job well," Lauren snapped, too forcefully. Then, afraid she had wounded his feelings again, she avoided his gaze and admitted slowly, "But you're uncomfortably close to the truth. It's easier to do my work if I'm more mature than my clients."

"A middle-aged couple on the brink of divorce tends to think of you as a whippersnapper who hasn't seen enough of life yet, hmm?"

He was very perceptive, Lauren noted. Intrigued even more by this engaging but unsettling man and his unique mixture of quick quips and shy manner, Lauren asked, "Do they teach psychology in computer classes?"

His answering smile was rueful this time. "I'll tell you

a secret, Doctor. I've given up trying to look and act older for the benefit of other people."

"Do you think I'm doing that?"

"Aren't you?"

"It's not . . ." Lauren gave up the argument. "I like being an adult. And I have a professional career to live up to. You can understand that, I'm sure."

"Of course," he said blandly. "But you're only thirty-one."

"And . . . ?" Lauren asked, knowing he had more to say.

Gallagher shrugged. "Maybe I'm in a different position than you are . . ."

"Not so different," Lauren shot back without thinking.

"Okay," he said suddenly. "Look, a couple of years ago I decided I was missing a lot of fun by trying to measure up to the preconceived notions of the rest of the world. I shouldn't have to be old before my time. There's too much to enjoy. I do as I please now. People think I'm a little eccentric, maybe, but who cares?"

"I'm not missing any fun, thank you," Lauren countered, and she swiftly began to gather up the litter of their shared meal. "Don't worry about me, Mr. Gallagher."

He watched her clean up, perhaps considering an apology for what he had just said. Instead, however, he told her abruptly, "You can skip the Mr. Gallagher bit. It makes me feel like a teacher when people call me that."

"What then?" Lauren snapped. "Finnegan T.? It's a wonderful name, mind you, but enough syllables to choke a horse."

His smile was genuine. "Finn."

Lauren met his look and felt her insides melt just a little. He had such a nice smile—open and honest and just a bit boyishly crooked. Lauren hesitated, then put out her hand for a formal shake. She said softly, "Finn, then. I'm Lauren."

He took her hand, his own warm one closing over hers in a grip that was wonderfully firm yet gentle. Erotically gentle. He held her lightly, but he shook his head with decisiveness. "Maybe you're Lauren to your clients and your

esteemed colleagues. I like you like this—young and pretty
and clever. With a smart mouth but a fear of hurting my
feelings. I think you're a Laurie."

Lauren nearly objected, but was suddenly acutely aware
that she could feel his pulse in her hand. Her heart seemed
to jump and speed up, a swift counterpoint to his more
measured beat. A dryness came to her throat, and Lauren
felt abruptly—pleasantly—lightheaded. She swallowed hard
and wondered what he was thinking.

"Yes," Finn said quietly, his eyes never leaving hers.
His smile grew intimate. "Definitely a Laurie. I used to
have an aggie the color of your eyes."

Lauren laughed, but the sound wavered and evaporated
too quickly. She said, "What a claim to fame! What happened to it? Lost with the rest of your marbles?"

"It's probably still in my old room at home. My parents
never throw away anything." He loosened his grip on her
hand belatedly, but did not let go. "What time is it?"

Lauren collected herself, throwing off the momentary
loss of self-control, and checked her watch out of reflex.
"Oh, Lord! I've got to get back!"

"Never fear," Finn said. "Steve graduated from an amazing driving course taught by Italian-terrorist commandos,
and he can get this car to spin on its nose if he wants to.
There's plenty of time."

"I'm not sure—"

But he interrupted, "Plenty of time for this at least."

His grip changed, went around her wrist, and suddenly
he pulled, drawing Lauren across the seat. He sat back and
pulled her slender body to him. She didn't fight, didn't
think, and suddenly she was in his arms and bracing her
free hand against his chest out of surprise. Lauren lifted her
mouth to speak, to object, perhaps, but he was there, taking
the kiss long before she thought of giving it. He slipped his
hand behind her head and tipped her up, making the coupling
of their mouths firmer, more sensual.

He was warm and hard and smelled faintly, surprisingly,
of the sea. He kissed her tentatively, uncertainly, not hurting. He didn't push her back into the seat with the skillful

move of a makeout artist, but let Lauren ride easily against his chest. Her body molded instinctively to his.

It was like a kiss between youngsters in the back seat of a car at twilight, instinctive and unpracticed, and yet packing an overwhelming jolt of excitement. Without thinking, Lauren slid her hand up to his throat and then around to the back of his neck. His skin radiated an inner warmth, and his hair was thick and curling in her fingers. Foolishly, she slipped her hand up farther, and placed it more securely around his neck.

At her exploring touch, Finn deepened the kiss and sought to part her lips, but only far enough to test their softness, her willingness. Gently, he let go of her wrist and dropped his hand to her hip in a feather-light caress.

Lauren heard herself sigh as she gave in to the unexpected flow of satisfaction that swept up from within her body. This was new. This was delightfully gentle, pleasantly child-like.

And therefore perhaps calculated. With a tug of regret in her heart, Lauren broke the sensual kiss. An unsteady breath left her body, and she eased back, slipping away from him.

Finn let his hand slide from her hip. "You see?" he murmured thoughtfully. "Isn't it nice to act your age again?"

"Goodness," she breathed, her fingers on her suddenly sensitive lips.

"Surprised yourself, didn't you?"

Lauren knew that her eyes were wide on his. "What am I doing here with you?"

He laughed. "Being yourself, I think. You don't have to be grown-up and sophisticated with me, Laurie. You played baseball this morning, remember? Nobody else in that crowd even considered joining in. And I bet you've kept that daisy, haven't you?"

"I—I've got to get back."

After a moment of regretful hesitation, he said, "Sure. But if you want to throw all your cares away and run off with me sometime, I think we'd have fun."

chapter 4

IT WASN'T GUILT that delivered Lauren to the doorstep of Interface on Wednesday morning. It was a moral obligation, she decided.

"You're really going to do this?!" Billy demanded in disbelief. "You? The busiest single lady in Baltimore?"

"I feel obligated!" Lauren cried, holding his hand firmly in her own. "Maybe I should have investigated more carefully—I mean actually experienced a computer dating service before I wrote about it. All those interviews with other people were enlightening, but maybe I should have done it myself."

Billy was digging in his heels, fighting Lauren as she pulled him along. "Sounds to me as though Gallagher twisted your arm."

"No," Lauren said decisively, shaking her head. "He is definitely not the arm-twisting type."

"Oh?" Billy asked, suddenly interested. "Just what type is he, may I ask?"

She sighed and faced Billy as they halted in front of the

Interface door. "Believe it or not, I think he's the lost-puppy type. A Great Dane puppy, mind you, but he's got this— this funny kind of innocence that's—I don't know! It's different, that's all." She reached for the doorknob.

"Oh, gosh," Billy moaned. "Another man for you to mother!"

"I am *not* mothering him! I'm not even going to see Finn on a social basis! He simply—"

"Finn?" inquired Billy. "You're calling him Finn now?"

"I can't be expected to reel off two dozen syllables all the time, can I? Are you coming or not?"

"Have I got a choice? You're going to fire me if I don't go along with this scheme of yours."

"I will not fire you, Billy."

"I know, I know." Billy laughed a little and stopped her, keeping them both in the hallway a moment longer. "I don't mind, really. I enjoy seeing you like this."

"Like what?" Lauren asked suspiciously.

Billy shrugged. "I'm not sure. The old gleam is back in your eyes, if that makes any sense. If this lapse in your strict, by-the-book attitude is caused by sweet, adorable Finn—"

"Oh, for heaven's sake!" Lauren burst out.

"He's a nice change of pace, that's all," Billy intervened smoothly. "Josh Redmond was nice, but definitely lacking in imagination, if you'll forgive me saying so."

"He hasn't died, you know."

"Hmm. Well, since his departure, you've been going to the opera with snooty Jeremy Blythe for example, not to mention your tour of French museums with that other foreign character with the mustache last fall and—"

"A trip to Hamburger Heaven with Gallagher the Whiz Kid is healthy, is that it?"

"Can't hurt," Billy said with a grin. "As I said, I'm getting a kick out of it."

"Let's see how much of a kick," Lauren said firmly. She pushed through the door and drew Billy along by the hand. "Are you ready to join Interface, my friend?"

Billy hadn't been easy to convince. He was darned unwilling, in fact, to join the dating service and subject himself to the resulting tortures. But he hadn't liked the idea of Lauren entering the lion's den alone, so he tagged along and signed on the dotted line. Together, they went through the process of joining Interface.

The receptionist, a cheerful red-haired young woman with a toothpaste manufacturer's dream for a smile, gave Lauren and Billy the canned speech as they filled out the initial applications.

"Interface is an international personal-introduction service that promises complete confidentiality," she explained to them. "We devote exact and personal attention to each individual member. We want you to be satisfied with our service, so please tell us if you're unhappy with anything you encounter today. Good communication is essential for success."

Billy had been filling in his name and his pen ran off the page, for he hadn't taken his eyes from the lovely redhead as she delivered her remarks. He smiled at her and said, "We won't argue with that, will we, Lauren?"

"Hmm?" Lauren asked, not looking up from her own paper. When Billy did not respond again, she glanced up to find him dreamily staring at the Interface receptionist. Lauren concealed a smile. Perhaps this experience wasn't going to hurt Billy's social life, either.

From the cheery reception area, Lauren and Billy were escorted to separate and private conference rooms where Interface counselors greeted them and began the confidential, in-depth interview. As Lauren settled into a comfortable armchair, she made a silent vow to cooperate completely with the interviewer. She was going to give this silly company a fair shake if it humiliated her beyond her wildest fears. Finn Gallagher—with his soulful eyes and shy smile—was going to get his money's worth out of this experiment, no matter what.

The interview began with easy-to-answer questions. Age and education and "deep background" questions like what kind of town Lauren was raised in and whether or not she had any pets as a child. Habits: Did Lauren smoke? No.

Drink alcohol? Occasionally. Leisure-time activities? Outdoor sports of nearly every kind, plus listening to jazz, reading historical romances, and hiking down the beach to the nearest ice-cream shop for a splurge. Favorite movies? Oldie-but-goodie romantic comedies. Later, Lauren would decide that such questions were designed to put the new member at ease with the interviewing counselor. Lauren did relax, for the young woman who sat opposite her at an unobtrusive computer terminal was pleasant and friendly, laughing with Lauren when her responses were less than serious.

From that point, the questions became harder to answer, and Lauren had to think carefully before she could reply honestly. What characteristic did she like most about herself? If she could change something about her personality, what might it be? What quality did she cherish most in a friend? What qualities in a person of the opposite sex did she find off-putting?

Then, worse yet: How would she react if her first Interface date asked to sleep with her? What part of lovemaking gave her the most pleasure? What was her ultimate fantasy? These sticky questions required quick thinking and tactful answers. Lauren found that her palms were sweating by the time this intimate line of questioning was over.

"Don't forget," the counselor reminded her gently when Lauren balked at the question about her ultimate fantasy, "these responses will never be seen by anyone but me and the computer, and after you're in the system, I'll never see this information again. Still, if you'd rather not answer, I'll understand."

"How about if I make up something?" Lauren asked nervously.

The counselor laughed. "Isn't that what fantasies are all about?"

So Lauren capitulated and made up a yarn about Scottish lords on white horses escaping across misty moors with her devoted assistance, and let it go at that. Sometimes those historical romances came in handy.

In time, the counselor sat back from the terminal. "I

think that covers everything, Dr. Chambers. You'll be protected by Interface, of course. We do not give your name to mailing lists or to anyone else, not even to the men who are members. The procedure is low key: You will receive a computerized list of potential partners—that means men who fit the profile indicated by your answers to this questionnaire. Though we have thousands of members in Interface, the computer will limit its suggestions to less than a dozen candidates."

"A dozen?" Lauren asked, "Local men, or will this be an international list?"

"Oh, local, at first. The computer is very picky. Then after you've had an opportunity to look over the profiles of the unnamed men, you contact us with a list of the members you'd consider meeting at a party arranged by Interface. The men are given a similar opportunity to narrow their field of possible candidates, and the computer coordinates the results. In time, the computer gives us a guest list, and we throw a party."

"What kind of party?" Lauren asked doubtfully.

"They're usually quiet affairs," the counselor assured her quickly. "We find that the average Interface member prefers a cocktail-hour meeting with the option of leaving early if he or she feels uncomfortable. Then we usually have some non-interaction activity, like a movie screening, perhaps a guest speaker, or a musician. Last month we invited an actor who was performing at the Kennedy Center in Washington to come here and give a poetry reading. He was wonderful! The Interface members can leave after the cocktail hour or stay as long as they like. It's very unstructured. We try to be as undemanding as possible. If you meet someone you like, that's great. You take it from there."

"Then you don't actually set up one-on-one dates?"

"Oh, no. We simply provide the opportunity for you to meet people who have similar profiles. If you don't meet anyone suitable right away, you will continue to receive the computer-tabulated profiles each month and invitations to more parties."

The interview had been long and intensive—nearly two

hours—and Lauren found herself thinking over her answers as she rode the bus out to her condominium that evening. It had become clear to her that Interface was in the people business, and they certainly tried to make prospective new members comfortable. Billy, for one, had been positively delighted with the set-up. He was gung ho all of a sudden. Lauren's own reaction was to feel strangely nonplussed. She was neither enthused nor disgusted. She hoped that she was keeping an open mind.

She realized that the biggest hurdle to be overcome in joining a dating service was the decision to join in the first place. Because of Finn Gallagher, she had been spared that trauma, but Lauren acknowledged that some single women and men might agonize for months before joining a group like Interface.

She changed into her scruffy jeans when she got home. To the music of her favorite Washington-based jazz radio station, she stir-fried a quick Chinese dinner for herself. Then, slinging an old sweater around her shoulders, Lauren carried her plate out to the sun deck for some solitude. She had to think over the day's events before she could decide how she felt about Interface.

Her apartment complex overlooked the water, and as the season began to warm up, Lauren enjoyed her evenings outdoors. The breeze off the Patapsco River, an inlet of the Chesapeake Bay, was crisp and pungent, a nice change after a day in the city. Lauren put on her sweater and settled back in her lounge chair to eat and watch the water. A sailboat bobbed idly out in the bay, and Lauren wondered if its owner was enjoying a pleasant supper before setting sail for home.

Her quiet reverie was interrupted by the telephone, and she went through the sliding glass doors to answer it. Her voice was cool and professional when she put the receiver to her ear. "Yes?"

"Hi," said Finn, sounding very far away.

"You again!" Lauren breathed, identifying him and abandoning her psychologist-on-the-line tone of voice. A funny thrill of pleasure caught her unawares, and she quickly clamped her arm around her waist to quiet the sensation.

"How did you get this number? I'm unlisted."

"I know you are. But I'm a computer genius, don't forget. I'll only be a minute, and I promise to forget your number immediately."

Lauren felt she should have been annoyed in addition to being curious about his methods, but she found that she was smiling instead. Glad that he couldn't see her, she asked, "Are you checking up on me? Making sure I'm going to go ahead with your request?"

"You already did," Finn answered with a laugh. "I see you've enrolled in Interface. How do you like it so far?"

"What do you mean you see I've enrolled?"

"I'm tied in to their computer, of course. You're—"

"What else can you see?" Lauren demanded, remembering all the very personal questions she had reluctantly answered for the Interface computer. "You don't have all the information they took from me today, do you?"

"Sure. Every word."

"But that was supposed to be confidential!" Lauren cried. "And the woman who interviewed me vowed that no one else would ever see that stuff except the computer!"

"She was right. Absolutely confidential. Except that I own the computer, so I occasionally have a look when something interests me. It's all right. I'll never repeat any of this stuff. You've got a real love for chocolate and Scotland, haven't you?"

"Oh, murder!" Lauren exclaimed.

He laughed again, or maybe the telephone connection was bad, but Lauren couldn't hear what came next. She jiggled her own receiver and demanded, "Where are you? In Scotland yourself? You sound oceans away."

"Oceans?" he repeated, sounding very amused. "No, but I am out of the house. The connection's fuzzy. Can you hear well enough?"

Remembering the mobile phone in his limousine, Lauren nodded and pulled the phone with her, walking to the glass doors again and leaning there in the wafting breeze. "Well enough, I guess. What did you want? To rub it in that you know all my personal secrets?"

"No," Finn said, and then he asked, "Are you mad at me?"

"Mad?" she echoed with sarcasm. "Why should I be?"

"Disgusted with me? Annoyed? Vowing never to see me again as long as you live?"

"For checking my answers on today's questionnaire? Yes, dammit!"

"And for the other thing?"

"What other thing?"

"In the car. I kissed you. Or you kissed me. Whichever it was, you were embarrassed about it. You pretended to admire the scenery the whole way back to your office."

"I did not!"

"All right," he agreed mildly, losing the argument with good grace. He asked, "Are you still?"

"Embarrassed? Yes, but not mad." Lauren was especially relieved that he could not see her face. She was blushing like a kid, and it was infuriating. Taking a deep breath, she said, "Boy, but you've got a quick way of getting past the preliminaries!"

"Preliminaries? Oh, I see. No, I just observe a lot. I'm awkward when it comes to actually interacting with people."

"You've done surprisingly well, as far as I can see," Lauren said dryly. She found that she was twisting her hair and abruptly hooked the offending strand behind her ear.

"Beginner's luck," he said, surprising the heck out of Lauren with that remark.

"Are you a beginner?" she asked, laughing suddenly. "I was starting to think you were the smoothest come-on artist I've ever met!"

"No kidding?" he asked, seemingly pleased. "I hate to disappoint you, but I'm a rank amateur. What you see is what you get with me."

"Not always," Lauren cracked. "The Texas accent is gone, so I'm wondering what costume you're wearing at the moment."

"Fantasize," he suggested, evading her question with a deft change of subject. "Listen, I've done a terrible thing today, and I'm calling to apologize, even though unless I tell you you'll never know what I've done."

"Is this conversation making sense now?" Lauren inquired lightly.

"To me it is. Can you hear all right?"

"Yes." Lauren dragged the phone cord with her and went back out to the sun deck. She sat down in the lounge chair again and propped her feet up comfortably, preparing to listen. The sailboat hadn't moved yet, and she watched it without really noticing it as she spoke. "Go ahead," she said to Finn. "You were about to confess something."

"Yes." He paused as if organizing his thoughts for a moment and apparently chose to come clean. "I thought about you last night. I wondered about you. So today I invaded your privacy and learned your life's story."

"The Interface questionnaire. Yes, you already told me—"

"And a few other sources," he interjected carefully, sounding nervous.

"Earth to Gallagher. Unscramble that last transmission, please."

"I used the computer," he explained, and his voice was reluctant and tense. Steeling himself for her reaction, Finn stumbled ahead quickly, "I—I looked at your medical records and your tax returns and your telephone bill and your travel agent's—"

Lauren sat up as if she'd been zapped with an electrical current, and she grabbed the receiver with both hands. "Are you kidding?"

"No, it's the truth. I know it was wrong. I shouldn't be doing that stuff anymore. But it was a natural curiosity, and it's occasionally nice to know that I've still got the right instincts for snooping in the—"

"You sneaky fink!" Lauren exploded, the fury welling up in her with a great surge.

"I know it's terrible. I feel very guilty, so I thought—"

"That's just horrid! I can't believe anyone could do that!"

"It's a crime, in fact, so if you're inclined to have me arrested, I wouldn't blame you. But since it's impossible to detect whether or not I've been breaking in—"

"That's a terrible invasion of privacy!" Lauren exclaimed, truly angry now. She stood up in shock and her voice cracked. "How could you do such a thing?"

Very simply, Finn said, "I liked you."

"What?" she demanded, unable to believe her ears.

"I did," he insisted. "I thought about you all night, in fact. You're very nice, did you know?"

"Oh, for crying out loud—"

"I know, I know. You're dating half a hundred men in Baltimore and that guy in Chicago, so—"

Lauren collapsed back down on the chair. "H-how do you know about Charles?"

"Is that what the 'C' stands for? I should have guessed. Yes, I picked him out of the airline-reservations lists. You've been seeing him since last winter. I figure you met him on your trip to Vail."

Lauren didn't respond. She couldn't.

"You're angry," Finn said. "You've got a right. I'm sorry. I could have kept this a secret from you, but I've got a very guilty conscience sometimes."

"What else did you find?" Lauren demanded, her voice sounding cold and very hard. Her heart was pounding, and she had to force her body to relax.

"You don't really want to know."

"Yes, I do, dammit, and I've got a right! Tell me this instant!"

There was a short pause then, and finally Finn said with caution, "Nothing earth-shattering. You like the ocean."

"You learned that from Interface."

"Yes. You're a season-ticket holder for the theater group."

"I didn't mention that to Interface! How did you—what else have you found?"

"You took a course in Chinese cooking at the college. You got a speeding ticket in Pennsylvania last fall. I think you must have been on an antique-buying trip with somebody, but I didn't bother finding out who. Whoever it was, you shared a motel room in Lancaster."

"That's none of your business!" Lauren snapped. She didn't have to explain she had gone with Gloria, that was for sure! She was darned if she was going to satisfy Finn's perverted curiosity about a perfectly innocent weekend with a girl friend! Let him think the worst! "What else did you learn?"

He was warming to the subject then, for he sighed and added with relish, "I'll bet you didn't know your phone was tapped two years ago."

"Are you making this up?"

"Sounds crazy, I know. The FBI was supposed to tap a line that had two digits different from your number. It was a fluke, but they didn't catch it for a month. Amazing."

"My God, how can you find out that stuff?"

"It's all in the knowing how. Are you furious?"

"Of course I am!" Lauren cried. She faltered. "And—and—"

"And you're scared, too." He was quick on the uptake and extremely accurate as usual. He must have heard the timbre of her voice change and quaver, for he said, "I'm sorry. Really I am. It was fascinating after a while, though, and I meant no harm. I'm not an ax murderer."

"This is very creepy," Lauren murmured, half to herself. She huddled on the lounge chair as the darkness closed in around her and added softly, "I *am* scared."

"It's okay," he soothed. "Why would I tell you if I was going to do something bad? I was just interested, that's all."

"What do you think you've accomplished by all this?"

"I got to know you better. Some people can talk and get acquainted easily, but I'm not good at that social stuff. I say the wrong thing and upset people—women, mostly. This was a better way for me to ask all those questions men are supposed to ask women directly."

"What for? Where are you going with this?"

"I told you," he said patiently. "I like you. I think you're nice. I think we'd have fun together."

"Are you suggesting—?"

"No, no," Finn said hastily, backing down like the Cowardly Lion in *The Wizard of Oz*. "I'm not suggesting anything. Just think of me, that's all. And I'll come see you sometime."

"When?" Lauren demanded immediately. "Where are you?"

"You *are* frightened," Finn noted with regret.

"Are you outside?" Lauren asked, fearfully going to the edge of the sun deck and peering around the corner of the building to look at the parking lot. "Are you sitting in your car, near here?"

"No, no," he said gently, reluctantly. Then, "Let's forget it, all right? Forget I called."

"No, wait," Lauren cried, clutching the receiver close again. "Finn!"

He was silent, but he didn't hang up.

"Finn," Lauren said again, better controlled this time. "Please don't—look, just give me some time to get used to the idea, all right?"

"You sound as if you think I'm crazy and you're being the psychologist now," he murmured unhappily.

"Look," Lauren began swiftly, "when six months is over and I'm finished with Interface, we can—"

"Six months!"

"Of course. After I've completed this arrangement with Interface and written the article you asked—"

Suddenly, Finn broke in plaintively, "Wait a minute. What do you mean? You're not seeing anyone—dating any men during your enrollment at Interface?"

Surprised, Lauren said, "It would hardly be fair if I did, would it? I intend to make the fairest possible evaluation of your company, so I'll just keep my other friendships to a minimum during that—"

"But six months!" Finn objected. "That's half a year!"

Laughing, Lauren said, "Yes. It's a very short time, honestly. In the interim—"

"I don't think I want to wait that long."

"Mr. Gallagher," Lauren said firmly, "you have no choice in the matter. This is my decision. I have joined your dating service, and I will fulfill my obligation to you there. But as far as seeing you on any kind of a social—"

"I'm not talking about formal dates, y'know. Not going to the opera or antique-hunting on weekends. I just think you're going to disintegrate into a middle-aged shrink pretty soon if you don't have some fun. Laurie, can't we—"

"Lauren," she corrected. "No, Finn, this is it. Six months. My rules, all right?"

He didn't respond.

"Finn?"

Hesitantly, he said, "Yes?"

Lauren wasn't sure yet. Maybe Finn Gallagher wasn't an ax murderer, but he was certainly more than a little eccentric. He seemed harmless enough in person, but now Lauren had her doubts. Who knew what kind of trouble she could be getting into? But the memory of his sweet kiss in the back seat of his limousine asserted itself just then, and Lauren sighed unevenly. He couldn't be dangerous, surely. But best not to upset him or hurt his feelings, anyway. Lauren made her decision and said gently. "Thank you for telling me about what you did. It was—I appreciate your honesty."

"Okay," he said slowly. "You won't be frightened?"

"Maybe a little. It's all right. It's healthy."

He must have smiled, for there was relief in his voice when he spoke. "Okay. Turn on the lights and the television. That ought to make you feel very safe."

"How did you know the lights were off?" Lauren demanded.

"Oh, he said, sounding uncertain once more. "Lucky guess, I suppose. Good night."

chapter 5

THE FIRST INTERFACE party came with surprising speed. Lauren received her data from the computer, made her selections, and within two weeks received an invitation to a party.

Within those same two weeks, however, she heard not a word from Finn Gallagher. Lauren wondered if she had imagined his late-night phone call. Perhaps he had decided to leave her alone, after all.

"I have my doubts about this system of Gallagher's," Billy told Lauren as they rode up the elevator of a Baltimore hotel to the party on the top floor. His enthusiasm for Interface had begun to wane from the time the invitations had arrived at Lauren's office. Now that he was about to face a group of people, he was unnerved. He tugged at the stiff collar of his shirt and asked, "If Interface is so careful about matching up people, why am I invited to the same party you're invited to? We're supposed to be meeting a group of compatible people."

"You and I are compatible," Lauren argued, pushing

Billy's hands aside and tightening the knot on his tie herself. "Why shouldn't we be invited to the same party?"

"The only thing you and I have in common is our work," Billy said irritably. "Which leads me to believe that this room is going to be full of psychologists and social workers. Or, worse yet, graduate students. We're going to see all the people we work with year after year, and they're all going to think that we're incapable of finding a 'meaningful relationship' without the help of a damn computer!"

"Nonsense," Lauren said, and she gave Billy a comradely pat on his shoulder. "You've got the jitters, that's all. These people are in the same boat, aren't they? Why should we feel uncomfortable?"

"Everybody's going to be a loser," Billy moaned. "I just know it."

But Billy was wrong. The party was small—perhaps two dozen men and women ranging in age from their late twenties to early forties, and everyone appeared to be quite normal. Billy, however, took a fast look around and spotted the red-haired receptionist from Interface. She was pouring drinks at a bar in one corner, and he made a beeline across the floor. Lauren, left stranded, took courage in hand and plunged into the nearest group. In time, she recognized one of the men, and she fell into a pleasant conversation with him about his work as a public defender. Then everyone began to circulate, and the noise grew to a successful-party level.

And Lauren met Philip.

He was very nice, confident, attractive. Not witty, exactly, but he smiled at Lauren's lighthearted conversational gambits. He was an executive with a bank and he had moved to Baltimore six months ago.

"I wanted to get out and meet people," he confided to Lauren as they stood chatting near the windows. "But in the middle of winter, nobody in Baltimore sets foot from their own living rooms, it seems. I'm from Phoenix, and I wasn't prepared for the weather here! Joining Interface seemed to be a good idea."

Philip was pleasant company, besides being an attractive

man. He was above medium height, was obviously physically fit, and seemed relaxed in a social situation that Lauren had to admit she was nervous about. He asked polite but not overly personal questions of Lauren, and he told her a little about himself. He enjoyed his work and played racquetball now and then for exercise. He wasn't married, though he had been. He was divorced and had two children who lived with his ex-wife in Arizona.

"I do miss them," he said as he refilled Lauren's glass of wine. "I thought I was bearing the separation pretty well until my son's birthday last week. I felt so bad about missing it that I jumped on the first plane and went for a visit."

Lauren smiled at his honest admission and patted his arm supportively. She said, "It's good to be impulsive sometimes, isn't it? It keeps us young."

Philip agreed—with mild surprise at her nonjudgmental response to his confession, and from that point his interest in Lauren sharpened. He clearly enjoyed her company and appreciated her undivided attention. As for Lauren, she found that Philip reminded her a little of Josh—very businesslike and proper, but with an intelligence that made for good conversation.

Before their conversation could go much further, however, the evening's entertainment was announced. A few of the guests chose to leave then, but most stayed and prepared to relax into the comfortable chairs set around the room.

Billy appeared at Lauren's elbow, having been deserted by his redheaded friend. "Are they kidding?" he asked out of the corner of his mouth when he had slid to a stop beside her.

"What do you mean?" Lauren inquired as she took the seat that Philip was offering her.

"The entertainment, for Pete's sake! Were you too engrossed in your conversation to hear? It's a bagpiper!"

"A bagpiper?" Lauren asked in amused amazement. "Really?"

"Who books the acts for Interface?" Billy asked, rolling his eyes. "Somebody who loves Scottish customs, I guess, right?"

Lauren couldn't answer for a long moment. Scotland? A bagpiper? Who, indeed, hired the entertainment for the party? Had Finn anything to do with it? she wondered. With a firm shake of her head, Lauren decided she must have an overly active imagination. Surely Finn didn't get involved in this level of the company! Still . . . he had seen her Scotland response on the Interface questionnaire. Could the computer have chosen a Scottish theme for this party all by itself? Or was Finn lurking behind the scenes?

With uneasiness starting to nibble at her stomach, Lauren slowly sat back in her chair. The piper, dressed in full Scottish regalia, gave a short, serious talk about his music, and then he puckered up and started to blow. Bagpipes did not rank in Lauren's top ten of favorite musical instruments, but after the initial squeal and wail, she began to enjoy the unique sound. She tapped her toe along with the familiar tunes and smiled as she added her applause to that of the group. Nearly any kind of music appealed to Lauren, and the pipes were hauntingly lyrical.

Even Philip seemed to enjoy himself. Billy, on the other hand, visibly winced each time the piper launched into a new song. He fidgeted and sighed and looked bored, and he couldn't keep from peeking over his shoulder now and then. Looking for the redhead, Lauren guessed with a suppressed grin.

When the piper finished and took a bow, Lauren was relieved—for Billy's sake. He jumped to his feet, having spotted the receptionist as she came through the doors with the catering service in tow.

"I'm not really hungry, Lauren," Philip said as they got more slowly to their feet. "I'd prefer to skip the refreshments, to tell you the truth. Would you like to go somewhere? Perhaps for a drink?"

Lauren smiled. Why not? Making friends was precisely the purpose of joining Interface. She was about to respond to him, when a burst of laughter erupted from the doorway. Lauren turned to look, and so did Philip.

The caterer had gotten into the spirit of the evening, it seemed, by dressing the waiters in kilts. A young man came into the room bearing a huge glass dish over his head. If Lauren wasn't mistaken, the dish contained a fruit trifle, a distinctive Scottish dessert of cream and sweetened fruit. He did a little jig as he came into the room, flashing the hem of his kilt and drawing laughter from the party guests. Two more waiters followed, also in traditional Scottish dress.

Billy hooted with laughter at the costumes and led the applause.

Then, as the Interface guests began to follow the waiters to the tables, Lauren swallowed hard and stumbled. She caught her balance with a hand on the back of her chair.

There he was.

With a big smile, Finn Gallagher came sailing into the room, dressed just like the others in a dashing red-plaid kilt, a crisp white shirt with a cute little tie, a pretty velvet jacket, and a jaunty hat with a curling feather, which he snatched off as soon as he set foot into the room. His long legs were encased in high argyle socks that had ribbons fluttering around his knees. A scabbard—good grief, could he possibly be *armed?*—clanked against the oversized safety pin on his kilt. His smile was bright and full of devilment as he locked his eyes with Lauren's.

"Oh, dear," she breathed nervously, bracing herself.

Philip took Lauren's elbow to steady her from behind. "Are you all right?"

"Y-yes," she said quickly, unable to tear her gaze from Finn's wickedly sparkling eyes. "I—I hope so, anyway."

"You're not going to faint, are you?"

Something far worse than fainting was going to happen, Lauren suspected, if she didn't get out of here before that look on Finn Gallagher's face resulted in some real mischief. If he wasn't above snooping into confidential computer records, Finn was certainly brave enough to try anything. "No, I won't faint," Lauren said to Philip. "But the drink you suggested might be a very good idea right now."

"I'll be right back," Philip promised, misunderstanding Lauren's sudden loss of composure. "Don't move."

Before Lauren could stop him, Philip had hurried off to get a glass of something to revive her.

And Finn came strolling over, looking as pleased as a cat that had just slipped into a dairy. He took Lauren's hand and bowed over it. "Good evening, Doctorrr Chamberrrs."

Lauren nearly burst out laughing at his attempted Scottish accent. She mastered her face just in time, though, and demanded, "What kind of shenanigans are you up to, may I ask?"

Finn must have felt the quiver of delight in her hand, for he smiled into her eyes and plunged ahead with his Scotsman's burr, "Shenanigans, you say? Don't you trrrust me, Laurrrie?"

"Lauren," she corrected in laughing exasperation, tugging her hand from his. "Of course I don't trust you! You're up to some trick, I can see."

"Ah, neverrr fearrr, fairrr lassie. I've come to whisk you away—to rrrescue you frrrom this deadly place."

"Deadly? Finn, I—"

Finn tipped his head close to hers and, with a wink, confided, "Deadly dull, I mean. Come along, fairrr lass. My horrrse is waiting."

"Finn!"

But he shot a furtive glance around the place, like the clan scout about to sneak a Scottish princess out from under the noses of the king's men. He was playing his part to the hilt. Then he seized Lauren's hand and without explanation began to drag her across the room, heading for the door.

Philip came out of the throng of party guests, a glass of wine in one hand and a startled expression on his face. He took a look at Finn's outlandish outfit and faltered to a stop, staring. In wonder, he glanced at the captured maiden and politely inquired, "Lauren . . . ?"

Finn spun Lauren protectively behind him with a technique that would have done Errol Flynn proud. Then, with a battle cry, he made as if to whip his sword from his scabbard to defend her. But the thing stuck, and he ended up yanking the blade out with both hands in a comical show of ungainly arms and legs. Weapon raised, he called, "Stand back, sirrr, orrr I'll be forrrced to defend the lady with my life!"

Some of the guests began to laugh, applauding the show, but Philip stood stock still, absolutely baffled. Two waiters, joining into the spirit of the performance, leaped forward to assist Finn, one brandishing a cocktail fork as a weapon, the other with his hands uplifted, karate style.

"To arrrms, men!" Finn shouted, backing out the door and pushing Lauren along. "Coverrr my escape!"

He kicked the door closed and caught Lauren up under her arm. He was running, or nearly, dragging a helplessly giggling Lauren every step of the way to the elevator. They dashed in together, and Lauren fell against the back railing, laughing. Finn punched a button on the control panel and turned, a big smile on his face and the sparkle of fun still in his dark eyes. "Well?"

"You're crazy!" Lauren burst out in amazed hilarity. "You're absolutely nuts!"

"Professional opinion, Doctor?" Finn asked, bowing over his sword in the fashion of a victorious pirate captain. His smile was delighted as he straightened up again and absorbed the expression on Lauren's face with glowing eyes. "Or wishful thinking?"

"Just a lucky guess," Lauren shot back, still amused, as the elevator began to descend. "Why on earth did you wreck your own party with a stunt like that?"

"Stunt?" Finn demanded, feigning outrage. He collapsed against the side of the elevator. "I just risked my life to rescue you from terminal boredom! I could catch pneumonia wearing this skirt! I may be dead by morning!"

"What a way to go! The outfit looks just lovely, Finn." Smiling, Lauren sent a studious eye down the length of his kilt to the colorful argyles below. "The socks especially."

Finn followed her gaze, rolling out on the sides of his shoes in a bow-legged stance to have a look himself. "Do you like them? The ribbons are nifty, aren't they? I like things that are lively. Boredom drives me up the wall!"

"The party—if that's what you're talking about now—" Lauren said, "wasn't the least bit boring even before you showed up. It was very nice. In fact I—"

"Oh-ho!" Finn interrupted exultantly, straightening up

with a gleam in his eye. His hair—as wild as before—curled down over his brow in a devilish forelock. "So Interface isn't so bad after all?"

"Well . . ."

"You can't actually be enjoying your membership with Interface?" he demanded with a chuckle.

"It hasn't been too bad so far," Lauren admitted.

"Not too bad? That's practically a cheering endorsement coming from the lady who wrote a scathing magazine article so very recently."

Lauren's mood deflated with the speed of a popped balloon. She glared at him in suspicion. "Are you trying to prove a point?"

"A point?" he asked, testing the tip of his sword with a cautious finger. He jumped, as if pricked by the blade, and stuck his forefinger in his mouth to ease the pretended pain. Then he grinned. "The only points I'm trying to make . . . are with you."

"I hate being manipulated," Lauren warned firmly, "and what you're doing right now, Mr. Finnegan T. Gallagher, seems suspiciously close to—"

"I'm not the manipulating kind," Finn said quickly, sheathing his sword and giving up the masquerade.

"Then what—"

The elevator arrived in the lobby of the hotel. Finn took Lauren's hand in his with a swift grab. "I'm just having second thoughts about putting you through such an awful experience, that's all."

"Interface is awful?" Lauren objected, too surprised to resist as Finn pulled her out into the lobby.

"You didn't meet any nice men, did you?"

"That's the whole point of—"

"You didn't meet anyone as nice as me, did you?" he asked anxiously.

"If I didn't know better," Lauren said with a sudden burst of illumination, "I'd say you were jealous of the men I'm meeting through Interface!"

"I *am* jealous," Finn said matter-of-factly, drawing her across the carpeted floor.

"You can't possibly think—"

"Interface isn't your style," Finn said quickly, turning to face her and walking backward at the same time. He waved to the desk clerk and kept going. "It will be dull for you. No fun. Stifling. It's not healthy. You've already seen that the parties aren't full of weirdos and dirty old men scouting nubile young girls, so now you can safely believe that the company isn't—"

"Finn Gallagher!" Lauren dug in her heels, hauling Finn to a grinding stop in the middle of the lobby. "You're trying to get me to quit, aren't you?"

Finn blinked in surprise. "Of course."

"After all you did to convince me I should join Interface?"

"I shouldn't have threatened you. I withdraw the request."

"So that I'll spend my time with you instead?"

"Yes, exactly."

"Look," Lauren began firmly, though her voice had begun to shake with growing anger, "I've made a commitment to this thing, and I'm not going to back out because you've decided you'd like to spend a few evenings in my company."

"It doesn't have to be evenings," Finn said quickly. "We can do all kinds of—"

"No!" Lauren objected, her voice echoing suddenly in the large lobby. Startled by her own vehemence, she glanced around nervously before facing Finn again. Lowering her tone, she said, "We agreed that I would participate in Interface for six months and give your company a fair evaluation. To keep an open mind, I've got to stop seeing men that I meet in other situations—"

"I don't think so," Finn argued gently, and he began to propel her toward the revolving door and the sidewalk beyond. "I'm not asking you to do something unnatural, Laurie, so you—"

"Lauren!" she corrected.

"And I don't think waiting six months is going to change my mind about you," he insisted. With surprising strength, Finn pulled her into the revolving door with him. Into the same compartment, in fact. "Forget about Interface and come with me."

"This is crazy!"

"No, just fun. Come on."

As he started to press through the door, pulling her with him, Lauren was forced to plaster herself up against Finn to keep from being crushed by the door. Here it was again, that queer bolt of lightning. He was a man, not a cartoon character in a silly costume, and Lauren was a woman, pressed against his body in a space not even as large as a phone booth. She bumped her knees against his and fought down the color that was already stinging her cheeks. "We hardly know each other, and you're hijacking me again!"

"It's more enjoyable than staying upstairs with the fuddy-duddy guy in the three-piece suit, I promise."

"Ouch! Finn, this is—" Lauren gasped for a breath and exploded, "How the hell do you presume to know what I might enjoy?"

"I think," said Finn, "that you enjoy this."

He braced his shoulder against the cylindrical wall of the revolving door and stopped it. *Whump!* The momentum drove Lauren hard into Finn's body.

They were trapped inside the door, and Finn slipped his arm around her shoulders. He pulled, eliminating the last millimeter of space between their two bodies, until Lauren's breasts were pressed firmly to his chest. Her legs tangled momentarily with his, and she sought to balance herself more securely—against him. Finn tipped her chin up with his other hand.

In the next instant, his mouth was headed for hers, and Lauren pinched her lips tightly together, determined not to let him kiss her. She jammed her hands on his chest and prepared to push. When his mouth touched hers, though, it wasn't rough or punishing, and the anger in Lauren's body faltered with indecision. Finn's lips were dry and gentle, uncertain perhaps, and definitely quick. He withdrew almost as fast as he had swooped in for the kiss, but he remained close, hovering.

Lauren met his dark but flickering eyes and felt her

willpower crumbling. She blinked to dispel the confusion of conflicting messages in her own mind, and parted her mouth to protest. The words didn't come, though. Finn's fingertips smoothed carefully along her jaw and found the downy softness of her hairline. He hesitated, watching her eyes, and then he ran his fingers gently through her hair. When he curved his hand around the back of her head, Lauren felt a woozy rush roll up from deep inside.

More slowly this time, Finn gathered her up and took her parted lips with his. He kissed her gently, slowly. Thoroughly. Then, with an unhurried, subtle gyration of his head, Finn parted Lauren's mouth just a fraction more. His tongue swiped a single, exploring stroke across her lower lip, tantalizing her with a warm yet questioning caress. It was as if he was asking permission, she thought dimly. He dared not push too hard. Yet under her hands, Lauren could feel his heart. It fairly thumped in his chest, a sign that his careful, measured restraint was manufactured. Did he even tremble once under her hands? Lauren laid her palm flat against him to check, a movement that Finn must have thought to be one of invitation. He moved his head again, that soft, rhythmic nudge that eased her lips wider, wide enough to let him in. Finn touched her tongue with his, and Lauren's knees went weak.

Despite her common sense screaming like a banshee in the back of her mind, Lauren began to kiss him back. Though she hadn't a clue as to why she was reacting this way, Lauren felt suddenly quite impatient. She slid her hand up his chest until she found his cheek. She laid her fingertips there, as if guiding him, showing him how the minute slanting of his head this way might perfect the pleasure, might heighten the sensuality. She let him savor the inner recesses of her mouth for a short time, and then she couldn't stop herself. She darted her own tongue across his firm lips and found herself teasing him, tasting him, encouraging him.

Finn slipped his warm palm securely around the nape of her neck and held her there inescapably, tilting her, manipulating the gentle motions of her head until he had regained command of the kiss. He eased one knee between hers. He bent her backward slightly, taking control of her slim body. The pressure of his arm around her shoulders increased, tightening until Lauren finally squirmed, her breath nearly squeezed from her entirely. Lightheaded, she tried to draw a breath. No use. A soft, plaintive moan escaped from her throat instead.

Finn let the power of the embrace diminish. He relaxed his grip upon her body and gradually set her down on solid earth once more. The contact of their mouths grew less and less intense until finally the wonderful sensation was no more than an imperceptible touch. Lauren opened her eyes.

Finn's gaze was dark and turbulent. He expelled a quiet, uneasy breath.

"G-good heavens," she whispered, unable to tear her eyes from his.

Finn swallowed, obviously as stunned as Lauren had been by the swift current of emotions that had just carried them away. He couldn't speak.

"I think," Lauren said thickly, "that we're blocking traffic."

He appeared to wake up then, and without further ado he pressed through the revolving door, pulling Lauren with him until they stood uncertainly, awkwardly, on the sidewalk. The evening air hit them like a bucketful of freezing seawater.

A small knot of people had gathered impatiently outside the revolving door—a baggage-laden cab driver and his two disgruntled passengers, a frowning hotel guest with a newspaper under his arm, and a woman who might well have been a member of the hotel housekeeping staff. Lauren blushed profusely as the group filed one by one into the just-vacated door. The woman, last in line, gave Lauren a benevolent smile before she scooted through the spinning doorway.

Finn dropped her hand and stepped back. "I'm sorry."

Lauren looked up at him, and the lump of tight happiness in her chest suddenly dissolved. Finn's face was blank with shock, slack with uncertainty, and Lauren felt her own facial muscles contract in response. He was upset.

"I—I'm very sorry," he said again. "I didn't mean to do that."

"What? Kidnap me? Or overwhelm me in a fishbowl with half of Baltimore watching?" Lauren glanced pointedly at the glass windows of the revolving door.

He flushed. "I—I should have known this would get out of hand."

"Out of hand?" Lauren repeated in amazement.

"I'm sorry," he said again, hanging his head to avoid her eyes. He looked uncomfortable. No, Lauren decided. He looked miserable. Unhappily, he sighed. "I'm such an amateur at this stuff."

"Amateur status doesn't quite define your particular brand of interaction," Lauren said bitterly. Now what? He was looking as if he'd just been stung by a live wire and hadn't recovered yet. Lauren watched his discomfiture with growing indignation. Did he have to make her feel so terrific one instant and then so thoroughly foolish the next? What did he think she was? Jezebel? A wanton nymphomaniac panting to exhaust him for life?

His head came up and he met her eyes. His face mirrored the tempest of emotions inside his head, and he swallowed hard. "Look, maybe you'd better go back upstairs. This isn't what I intended, and I'm sorry—"

"Just what did you intend?" Lauren asked, hugging her elbows. In her silk dress, she was chilled suddenly, and she began to shiver.

"I—I just thought we could be friends, that's all. I never meant—" Finn gave up his explanation and started to strip off his velvet jacket. "This is probably scary for you, and I really don't want you to think I'm as—as crazy as I'm acting at the moment. Here."

Lauren held still while he wrapped his jacket around her shoulders. She accepted the pretty garment, hugging the lapels tightly in her hands. One of them was crazy, that was certain. Hadn't he just given her the kiss of a lifetime? What was so bad about that? What had him so upset? "Finn . . ."

"It's okay," he said quickly. "I won't hurt you. I'm—"

"If you apologize one more time, I'm going to kick you

right in your argyles." Lauren pinned him with a lethal look.

His smile came quickly, but disappeared just as fast. "You're angry. You've got a right. I'll take you back upstairs, if you'd like."

"After the exit we just made, I don't think I'd enjoy going back to that group. I'd like to go home, thank you."

He nodded. "Did you drive? No? I'll get you a cab. Did you have a purse or something?"

"My coat and handbag are upstairs. Billy will get them for me, I'm sure. You've lost your little hat."

"Don't worry about it," he said, and he turned away and headed for the street.

He wasn't even going to drive her home! That kiss must have paralyzed his brain or something! He was petrified of being alone with her for another minute! Fuming, Lauren stayed on the sidewalk and glared at his back. She was angry, all right. He had just swept her away—without benefit of a white horse—in a scene right out of a vintage historical romance, and now he was dropping her as if she were the proverbial hot potato. Too hot to handle, huh? Was he afraid she was going to tear off his clothes or something?

He did look awfully cute in that kilt, she thought a moment later. His legs were long but not skinny, just muscled as if he ran or played some sport regularly. And his shoulders were broad and well toned under that handsome white shirt. Lauren found her imagination taking a nosedive, and she wondered what he might look like without—no. *No.* Don't panic him, Lauren, she chided herself silently. He reacted badly enough over one kiss!

But here was a taxi. Finn came shamefacedly back to claim her, but didn't risk taking her arm this time. "Here you go. The cabby says he'll take you anywhere you like, okay?"

Lauren nodded shortly and made as if to take off the velvet jacket. Finn stopped her with a gentle grip. "No, keep it."

His hand was warm and firm, and Lauren looked up into his face. There had to be something she—as a psychologist—could say to ease his obvious unhappiness. He was confused, perhaps frightened, and obviously torn about the natural sexual attraction between them. Lauren touched his arm. She said gently, "You know, Finn, being attracted to another person isn't bad. It's a healthy, human, sometimes wonderful reaction. You shouldn't have to fight against it, you see. It can be very nice, sometimes."

He didn't answer. Perhaps he didn't want to.

Lauren stretched up on tiptoe and gave him a soft kiss on the cheek. Then she went out into the street and got into the taxi.

chapter 6

IN THE CAB on the way home, Lauren tried to sort through all the possibilities. No doubt about it, she found Finn Gallagher attractive. He was so full of life! He was a fun-loving, earnest, boyish personality in the body of a desirable, sexually impulsive man. At least, she thought the kiss in the revolving door had been impulsive. Even Finn, with his unique way of looking at the world, couldn't have calculatedly planned that passionate embrace in the hotel doorway.

So why did he have to go and spoil it all by panicking like Benjamin confronted by an overly amorous Mrs. Robinson in *The Graduate?* Surely, a man his age had enough experience to enjoy a woman's natural response without fear for his safety! There had to be another reason for the way he'd reacted. Something—some realization, perhaps—had hit him like a ton of Scottish scones.

What was the use? Lauren had learned by her experience with Josh Redmond that a lady shouldn't lose her dignity while chasing a man. It just didn't pay. She had been hurt by Josh that way, and she didn't need to get the same treatment from this character.

The best medicine for her own problem, Lauren decided, was to try to forget about Finn Gallagher. If that was possible, of course. After all, it was tough not to try imagining in what guise he might show up next. In her mind's eye, Lauren pictured Finn dressed in countless outlandish outfits and spouting one crazy accent after another. Was there no limit to the man's eccentric behavior? Then he had to climax his performances by gathering her up and kissing the stuffing out of her. No, for sanity's sake, Lauren was going to have to try forgetting the peculiar Mr. Gallagher.

With that plan in mind, she accepted when Philip called later in the week with an invitation to go to a concert on Saturday evening.

"It's a benefit concert," Philip explained on the phone. "The visiting Boston Symphony conducted by John Williams. The proceeds will go to the Aquarium."

"Music to swim by?" Lauren asked with a laugh as she popped two M&M's into her mouth to suck on. She swiveled her chair around and propped her feet on the corner of her desk to relax before the next therapy session began. "Maybe they'll let the seals join the orchestra with those little horns they play?"

"Er—yes, that might be . . . enjoyable," Philip said doubtfully. "Would you like to go? It's formal dress, you see. And I've been asked to attend the reception afterward, also. The chairman of the bank's board is treating all the officers to supper at La Normanna."

Lauren recognized the name of the poshest restaurant in town. She wondered if she should break out her heirloom diamond necklace for the occasion. With her tongue, she maneuvered the candies into her cheek and said, "Why, yes, Philip, I'd like to go. It sounds like fun."

"Well," Philip had said dryly, "fun isn't exactly the word I might have chosen. The chairman of the board isn't likely to arrive in a kilt with a sword in hand. I'd enjoy your company, though."

"It's kind of you to ask me," Lauren said quietly, glad

that he couldn't see her discomfiture. Darn that Finn Gallagher!

"I have to call Interface and inform them that we'll be seeing each other Saturday night."

Lauren was startled and nearly choked on the chocolate that had begun to melt down her throat. "Inform Interface? Why, Philip?"

"Didn't they tell you? The man is supposed to report to the computer each time he sees a woman he's met through Interface. Sounds ridiculous, I know. But I'm a man who usually plays by the rules."

Lauren crunched the peanut centers of the M&M's thoughtfully. Then, with suspicion obvious in her tone, she said, "Nobody told me about that rule."

"I'm sure the company doesn't bother the women with such details. I'll take care of it. Is there something wrong with this connection?"

Lauren swallowed the last of her M&M's quickly. "Yes, I think so. The line sounds a little—um—crackly."

"Well, we may as well chat on Saturday, then. I'll pick you up at six-thirty, all right? Oh, and Lauren, the concert is being held outside. At Harborplace. Bring a sweater, just in case."

"I'll bring a sweater, and you bring an umbrella," Lauren said with a smile as she fished into her stash of candy one more time. "That way we'll be prepared, and it won't rain for sure."

"Why not?" Philip asked blankly.

"Because—well—" How could he be so dense? "It's sort of a superstition, Philip. If you wash your car, it's guaranteed to rain. If you carry an umbrella, it won't."

"Oh," he said. There came a long, uncertain pause, and then he asked, "Should I not wash my car, in that case?"

Lauren stifled a sigh. She was beginning to have her doubts about poor Philip. "Never mind, Philip. It was just a joke. I'll see you on Saturday, okay?"

"I'll be looking forward to it, Lauren."

That afternoon Lauren went out and bought a spectacular dress to wear for the upcoming occasion. It was a white shirtwaist with lovely, feminine sleeves that puffed around her shoulders, then cascaded down her arms in full, flouncy balloons of starchy cotton to end in dainty, buttoned-down cuffs at her wrists. A wide leather belt—very blue and soft to the touch—wrapped twice around her waist and cinched the summery dress to show off her slim hips. The neckline was prim and buttoned up tight, but—a pleasantly sexy surprise—the back of the dress was open, plunging down to the curve of her lower back to show off just a glow of early tan. She'd wear her hair tied with a ribbon—a blue one to match the belt—so that her long hair would tickle her bare back. It was a youthful outfit, Lauren decided. Pretty, but with a sexy dash. It ought to give the stuffy bankers at La Normanna a breath of summer air!

Pleased that she'd found such a unique dress, Lauren took a walk around Harborplace afterward to meet her friend Gloria Myla for their usual Wednesday lunch date. As she strolled along the quay, Lauren made up her mind that as soon as she could square things with her clients, she was going to take a vacation. Even a long weekend would be great. She'd set Billy to work on clearing the decks.

Gloria was already on their usual park bench, her face upturned to the May sunlight for a few minutes of tanning. Gloria had been Lauren's roommate through their graduate-school years, and now they remained good friends, often seeing each other during the week for lunch in addition to going to an occasional movie or on a weekend excursion together now and then. At least once every season they planned some kind of adventure together—the antique-hunting trip to Pennsylvania had been just such a trip. Gloria was a good travel companion. She never complained and had a unique ability to save her energy for the things that mattered most in life: hunting for the best restaurants and ferreting out the best buys in out-of-the-way shops.

Gloria didn't even blink when Lauren slid up and whispered, "Hey, lady, wanna see some French postcards?"

"Only if they're erotic," Gloria responded, in her usual deadpan fashion. It was hard to fluster good-old Gloria. She extended her hand to Lauren, who obeyed the silent command and pulled her friend to her feet. They hugged each other then, as was their custom.

The two women walked to a nearby ice-cream vendor and splurged for lunch with double-dip cones. Lauren ordered a scoop of chocolate-cookie ice cream with a scoop of rocky road on top and prepared to indulge while she spilled her story.

"What do you think, Glo?" Lauren questioned after she had told her friend about the party at Interface and the latest episode with Finn.

"Honestly?" Gloria asked, already attacking her ice cream with gusto. She sat back down on the bench, too sensible to combine the consumption of high-calorie delicacies with exercise even as mild as walking. Mouth full, she said, "I'll bet you dollars to jelly doughnuts that your Finn Gallagher has the computer rigged."

"You don't believe Philip's story that Interface wants all the men to register their dates with the computer?"

"Do *you* believe it? Of course not. Your Finn has given that line to Philip so he can keep tabs on you, right?"

Lauren sighed, staring out at the harbor. "Yes, I'm almost sure that's what's going on. Billy never heard of the rule, and he's a man."

"That's debatable," Gloria cracked.

Lauren caught a dribble of chocolate with her tongue before it could melt completely and land in a splotch on her skirt. She grinned at her friend. "You're still mad because Billy insulted your pork-roast glaze."

"You betcha. I'm not feeding Billy again until he apologizes." Gloria took a healthy crunch of her cone. "Your dilemma is infinitely more entertaining. My guess is that this Finn character already knows you're going someplace with Philip the fuddy-duddy. All he's got to do is figure out where you're going. I bet he shows up before the end of the concert."

"He wouldn't, would he, Glo?"

"Sweetie," Gloria said firmly, "the guy's had a week to calm down after you scared his hormones into the ozone layer."

"So?"

"So . . . by now he's probably dying to get you alone again and take advantage of a good thing. What man wouldn't, after you threw yourself at him like that?"

"I did not throw myself at him!" Lauren protested. "He was the one who trapped me in the door and started the whole thing. It's not like I'm the vamp of Baltimore, you know!"

"Couldn't prove it by me," Gloria shot back, seeming perversely pleased that she could ruffle Lauren's feathers. Gloria was a social worker with one of the county's youth agencies, and she didn't mince words when she got serious. "Listen, Lauren, just relax. Don't get bent out of shape over this."

"I am not—" Lauren stopped herself. Why, indeed, was she working herself into a lather over Finn Gallagher? Because of the way he could kiss her socks off, of course! Lauren wisely kept her thoughts to herself, however. Gloria didn't need to hear all the juicy details about her attraction to the lean and lanky Mr. Gallagher.

Having probably seen the signs of truth in her friend's face, nonetheless, Gloria said calmly, "Look, Lauren, if your Finn shows up at the concert, I think you ought to talk with him. Find out what his problem is."

"Why he panicked, you mean?"

Gloria nodded. "Maybe it was just some notion he's gotten into his head about you. It sounds to me as though he's got an inferiority complex of some kind. Talk it out, next time you see him."

"What if it's Saturday night and he's dressed up like a gorilla?" Lauren asked dolefully.

"Not for a benefit concert for the Aquarium," Gloria retorted with wry certainty. "He always dresses appropriately for every occasion. Look for a tall seal, or a shark with argyle socks. That'll be him."

"Oh, murder!" Lauren groaned. "I know half a dozen very nice men who'd like to escort me to perfectly sensible places this weekend, and I'm going to an outdoor concert for fish with Philip, the straightest banker since J. P. Morgan—only to keep my eyes open for a computer wizard dressed up for Halloween! What's gotten into me?"

"If I didn't know better," Gloria said blandly, "I'd say you were falling for one of them."

"Oh, for heaven's sake!"

"What else could it be?"

"Indigestion," Lauren said a moment later, eyeing her ice cream. "I think it's time I went on a diet, Glo. Before things get out of hand."

On Saturday morning, Lauren took a long bicycle ride to clear her head, and after a short snooze on the sun deck in the afternoon, she put on her new dress and waited for Philip to arrive.

When he appeared at her door, she invited him in for a glass of wine and some cheese and crackers. They chatted, and Lauren was pleased to find out that Philip was knowledgeable about Oriental silkscreens. He admired a print she owned, and expanded on the subject while they finished their snack. Then Philip suggested that they drive into the city.

Harborplace, a renovated section of downtown Baltimore, was resplendent with people, music, and the scents of a hundred delicious concoctions from nearby restaurants. The wide sidewalks and the spectacular esplanade of the nearby Aquarium were thronged with beautifully dressed concertgoers as well as the usual Saturday-night crowd that jammed the parklike area. Some yachts and a sleek sailboat or two were tied up at the quays. Streetlamps sparkled their lights on the water of the small bay, and the breeze was tangy with the smells of the sea.

The nip of excitement in the evening air tingled inside Lauren as she held Philip's arm and wandered through the crowd. She watched the happy people around them. She never tired of watching the habits of strangers. Half the city had turned out for the occasion of the Aquarium's birthday, it seemed.

Below the wide steps that led up to the Aquarium esplanade and the temporary seats that had been arranged for the concert, the crowd had gathered like slow traffic before a tunnel. As Lauren looked ahead to see how soon they might arrive at their seats, what she saw above them on the stairs made her gasp. Finn Gallagher, of course.

"Good Lord," said Philip, for he must have seen Finn at precisely the moment Lauren had. "Is that—?"

"Yes," Lauren replied, smiling in spite of her initial dismay. "Yes, it's him."

Finn was dressed this time in a wonderful black tuxedo, the kind with tails and a top hat. A crimson cummerbund showed through his open jacket, and his bow tie was also bright, bright red against the brilliant white of his sharply pleated shirt. His smile was just as much of a beacon as the outfit when his eyes met Lauren's over the heads of the people between them. He was standing on some kind of platform, she realized. Or maybe a box.

Beside him was a spectacular blonde, dressed in a dazzling silver lamé sheath dress, the kind that looked appropriate only at very formal occasions or on stage with the circus magician. It seemed that she was acting as Finn's assistant for this particular show, for she smiled and bowed to the concert patrons. She then made a flourish and displayed his cane to the crowd, a plain wooden stick that suddenly lit up like a red fluorescent bulb when Finn took it from her hands.

He waved it once, and produced a pigeon from nowhere. His audience cheered and clapped.

"What's he up to?" Philip asked glumly from beside Lauren. "I don't trust that character."

"He's harmless, Philip," Lauren said, watching the show. "Honestly, he is."

"He's not going to saw you in two, is he?"

"I think that's probably *her* honor," Lauren replied, indicating the lovely blond woman. She was very tall, and her figure was just as spectacular as her beautiful mop of fair curls. "I wonder who she is?"

"I'll bet it's not his mother," Philip said as Finn handed his assistant the white pigeon and she bestowed a delighted kiss on his cheek as a reward.

Applauding, the crowd edged away from the performers, giving them some elbow room, and the circle widened so that Philip and Lauren stood just eight feet away from Finn as he began the next trick.

"May I have a volunteer?" he asked the crowd. "Ah, here's just what I need! A lovely lady. Would you come here, please? Isn't she beautiful, ladies and gentlemen?"

Lauren blushed a furious red, but there wasn't time to jerk out of Finn's hand and run. Besides, the crowd was applauding and smiling and expecting a performance.

Finn led Lauren to the center of the circle and gave her his eerily glowing cane, smiling down into her eyes briefly. "Just hold this for me, will you? And count to ten very slowly. Sally, my hat, please!"

The people around her were laughing and enjoying the show, and Lauren felt she couldn't back out now. She held the cane up as Finn had showed her and began to count in a quavering voice. "One, two . . ."

"And now, ladies and gentlemen," Finn said from behind her. "With a little magic, I'm going to make this very pretty lady disappear! Abracadabra . . ."

Poor Philip never had a chance. One moment he was nervously watching from the sidelines, and in the next moment he was being dragged into the circle with his bewildered expression giving way to dismay. When Lauren last saw him, the statuesque blonde named Sally was curling her arm around his and smiling, complete with dimples, into his startled face. Then Finn whipped off his top hat, flashed a red scarf out of his jacket sleeve, and a huge white rabbit popped from the hat, squirming and wriggling. Finn dumped the rabbit into Philip's arms.

Then the cane in Lauren's hands began to vibrate like a living creature, and suddenly the top of it exploded! A puff of red smoke burst out, and instantaneously the whole circle was engulfed in red-colored smoke. Lauren squealed and dropped the cane, and then a strong hand closed over her arm. She couldn't see a thing, and could hardly breathe from the red smoke. She was dragged two uncertain steps, and then the crowd seemed to part like the biblical sea. She stumbled, but Finn's arm came swiftly around her back and he pulled her away.

They wove quickly through the cheering, laughing throng, Finn skirting this way and that and finally dodging clear. He made a break for it, dragging Lauren up a different set of steps to a darker sidewalk.

Lauren hurried to keep up with him, choking and hardly able to think straight for a few minutes. It didn't take Finn long to have her far out of sight. He pulled her by the hand around the corner of a warehouse, and suddenly they were alone. It was a private place, though very close to the crowd on the esplanade. It was quiet, too, except for the breeze off the harbor. They had left civilization behind. A single blinking light flashed from somewhere out on the water.

Common sense hit her like the cool wind, and Lauren twisted out of Finn's grasp. "That wasn't nice! Finn, I should go back to Philip. I'm supposed to be with him tonight!"

"He's going to be perfectly happy," Finn argued quickly, blocking her path by stepping hastily in front of her. His eyes were full of sparkle from the excitement. "Sally has a Ph.D. in international banking. They're perfect for each other!"

"Finn, you can't manipulate people's lives without their consent! I have to go back—"

"I'm not manipulating," Finn said, putting up both hands as if to prevent her words. "I did what Interface does every day. I introduced two compatible people. He's going to get a kick out of Sally, I promise. I looked all over the East Coast for her."

"Invading her privacy with your computer?" Lauren asked angrily.

"No," he said. "She's the sister of a friend of mine."

Lauren hesitated. Finn's face was again naked: open and full of hope, yet full of fear. A fear that she was going to leave him in anger? He didn't reach for her hand, as a more confident man might have done, but waited with touching anxiety for her to make her decision. Besides that, he looked adorable in his tuxedo and cute red tie.

Lauren had to look away. She put one hand to her face and rubbed, thinking. She sighed unevenly. "Oh, Finn!"

"It's okay," he soothed. "They'll enjoy themselves, I promise. Come with me."

"Where?" Lauren demanded. "The last time you started to hijack me, you decided to quit halfway through the thing! Are you going to drag me some place where you can dump me, and then go bolting off like a frightened—"

"I'm sorry I was so abrupt before," Finn said quickly. He put his hand out, asking permission to touch her. "I shouldn't have dropped you back to earth like I did. That scene in the revolving door at the hotel was—I just—" He shook his head, baffled. "It hit me, that's all."

Lauren took an automatic step toward him, even though her instinct was to keep back a little longer. He looked so pathetic that she took his hand gently and asked, "What hit you?"

"I just realized," he said, his voice going soft as he looked down at her hand and caressed the back of it with his thumb. "I realized when I kissed you then that I was falling in love with you."

"Ooooh, my goodness," Lauren breathed, staring straight into his eyes for a lightning bolt of a moment.

"Don't be frightened," he begged. He held onto her hand for dear life, as if afraid that she was going to run away if he let her go.

"Oooh, my goodness!" she repeated stupidly.

"Don't panic, ma'am," Finn drawled, diving immediately into one of his crazy disguises again. "I haven't got my smellin' salts with me."

"Oh, Finn!"

"It's nothing to worry about, darlin'," he soothed, holding her hand fast to his chest where his heart hammered below. "It scared the hell out of *me* at first, but you're s'posed to be an expert at this stuff."

"Finn, didn't you just say—"

"I've been thinking mighty carefully since I saw you last, Miz Laurie, and I jes' decided that I'm fallin' for you like a—well, like I haven't in a long, long time. There hasn't been a woman I've felt real strong about in a lot of years, and when it happened—"

"Honestly, Finn, if this is another of your silly acts, I'd prefer that—"

"It's no act, Miz Laurie, it happened so darn fast that I wasn't sure—I didn't know—I was afraid I was mistaking what I was feeling for—for a sexual kind of attraction and I—"

"Oooh, my goodness," Lauren moaned again, clapping one hand to her forehead.

"Not that I'm not sexually attracted to you," Finn added swiftly, abruptly giving up the phony Western accent. "I mean, you're very pretty, and I love the way you walk and the way you tip your face up to me when we talk, but I wanted to be sure my head was as—as excited about you as the rest of me was before—"

"You're really making this difficult for me, Finn!" Lauren burst out. "How am I supposed to—"

"Don't," he interrupted, pulling her bodily against him until she put her hand on his chest. Getting a fragile grip on himself, he pleaded, "Don't make any decisions about me yet, please? I'm really not crazy. I'm just not good at— at the same kinds of things that most men are good at. You don't know me well enough to say you don't want to see me anymore."

The conductor must have arrived on stage at the concert just then, for the eerie quiet of the night was broken by the distant sound of applause. The sound bounced strangely off the warehouse walls and the slapping water of the harbor, giving Lauren the impression that she and Finn were farther from the rest of the civilized world than they truly were. No one could hear them now, no one could interrupt. She was alone with him, and he had that miserable, lost-puppy look in his dark eyes once again.

Slowly, Lauren said, "I wasn't going to say that I didn't want to see you anymore."

"You weren't, darlin?" he asked, going Western once again.

"Of course not, Finn. I'd like to get to know you, but every time we meet, you're playing a different character! How can I know which one you really are?"

Suddenly, the strains of a Strauss waltz filled the night air, and the music brought a short, powerful lull to their almost whispered conversation.

Then, tentatively, Finn said, "You need some time. For me, it was—it was the first time I saw you that I knew you'd be perfect, Laurie. But you need to spend some—some normal time with me, okay? We need to talk without me being so silly anymore."

"You're not silly," Lauren said quietly. "You're just too fast for me, that's all. We've never—since the talk we had in the back of your car, you and I haven't really had a chance to just communicate like adults, have we?"

"Exactly," Finn said with relief.

"So . . . ?" Lauren prompted, helping him.

He smiled with pleasure. "So I thought we could spend tonight together and—" He caught himself, eyes popping wide comically. In a rush, he corrected himself, "No, wait—I meant spend this *evening,* not the whole night, of course. Together, I mean. Unless you want to spend the night with—well, I don't want to rush you."

"Thank you," Lauren said dryly.

"But," Finn said cautiously with a sideways look at her, "I do want to make love to you someday, Laurie. You know that, don't you?"

Lauren swallowed with difficulty. Sometimes—for all his bashful manner—Finn Gallagher could really floor her!

He slowly pulled her that last inch and held her lightly against his body. Perhaps it was only the music, but Lauren felt them both sway—very gently—in time to the lilting waltz beat. Finn seemed unaware of the rhythmic tune, however, and watched her face for signs of misgivings.

Shyly, he asked, "Will you forget what I told you? I should have saved that for later, I know, but I figured if I wasn't honest with you, I'd lose you before we even had a chance to start. I—I do love you, Laurie Chambers."

"Thank you, Finn," Lauren murmured, dropping her eyes

from his in a sudden rush of bashfulness. Good grief! He was turning her into a simpering ingenue! Get a grip, old girl! she lectured herself silently. Aloud, she said, "I appreciate your honesty. But I—"

"I know," Finn said hurriedly, flushing. "You don't feel the same way. It's much too early for you. That's understandable. Logical. Common sense."

"Thank you."

"You will forget I said it so soon, okay? I know I shouldn't have opened my mouth, but—I don't want to—if you—I mean—"

"I think it's fine," Lauren intervened, gathering her cool composure once more. It was an effort! Then, still held loosely in Finn's embrace, she sent a quick smile up at him. "It's a different approach, but it's fine. You have a way of flattering a woman that's totally unique, Mr. Gallagher."

"*Unique* is a word I've always disliked," Finn replied, his smile returning with his evident relief. He touched one finger to the fine wisp of hair that was blowing across her cheek and did not seem to notice that Lauren turned her nose so that he could brush the full length of her cheek with his fingertips. He explained, "Everybody describes me as unique, and right now I'd like to be as normal as—as that banker you came here with."

"Why would you like to be like stuffy old Philip?" Lauren felt a tiny twinge of disloyalty at characterizing Philip this way, but the words just seemed to pop out.

Finn smiled. His eyes brightened. He tipped his head like a suddenly alerted spaniel about to be sent after its favorite rubber ball. "Do you think Philip is stuffy? I thought you liked him."

Lauren laced her fingers more securely in his and slid her other hand just a few centimeters up his chest. Why, she wasn't sure. Lauren only knew that Finn needed reassurance, and this seemed the most natural way to give it. She said, "I *do* like Philip. He's a very nice man. I'll be angry if you've done something to upset or hurt him."

"I take care not to hurt anyone."

Lauren glanced up with a smile and found him watching

her. "I'm beginning to see that. I think I'll put it at the top of my list of your good qualities."

Finn smiled. There were any number of quick comebacks he could have made at that moment, but instead, he said suddenly, "I love waltzes, don't you?"

Lauren began to laugh. Finn wound his arm around her waist and drew her snugly against him. With her other hand captured, he spun her away into the darkness, perfectly in time to the distant tune. His first steps were flamboyant, a theatrical whirling with too-large steps that left Lauren breathlessly giggling and holding onto him for all she was worth to keep from falling. Then he seemed to catch himself and settled into a gentler waltz, as carefree as before but somehow more controlled, more comfortable. He swept her effortlessly around and around, heading toward the harbor with each revolution.

The music swelled magically around them. Lauren tipped her head back, as if to soak in the wonderful combination of melody and motion. Her hair flew around behind her, spreading the delicate fragrance of her subtle perfume into the air surrounding them. He was perfect. Finn danced with a real flair, never missing a beat and whirling her this way and that way, one-two-three, one-two-three. If she'd been wearing a hoop skirt, it would be sailing around them with the exciting momentum.

Smiling, Lauren wondered if the moonlight allowed Finn to see her expression of delight. He had infected her with his own brand of lunacy—she was angry one minute and completely charmed the next. This waltz was too enticing not to enjoy. Finn's arm was taut and strong behind her; his hand, so firm as it cupped the bare skin at the small of her back, felt warm and decidedly familiar. He found a niche just above the curve of her buttocks, and Lauren was aware that he could anticipate and therefore guide her dancing by that gentle touch. His hips met and ground provocatively against hers. His belly, arousingly taut and lean, rubbed pleasantly against her own.

He spun her once more with exuberant skill, and then faltered, yet somehow without breaking the rhythm. Lauren heard herself sigh, and she relaxed, nestling finally against his chest as their momentum lessened into a much more sedate dance. Throwing caution to the wind, Lauren laid her head against his neck. Their dance diminished further, until it was no more than a subtle motion of one body pliantly matching the infinitesimal movements of another. He smelled faintly like the salty sea air, and Lauren unconsciously inhaled that fragrance as it mingled with his own more elusive masculine scent.

The music faded, to be replaced by applause once again. Finn slowed even more, but did not stop. Together, they swayed in the breeze that blew off the harbor. Lauren held him close, glad he was so warm.

"Finn..." she murmured, as if testing how his name might sound when not spoken in exasperation for once.

His lips brushed the tender spot just below her ear. His voice was as soft as hers. "You make me shiver inside when you say my name like that."

She smiled, basking in the warmth of his body against hers. "Finnegan T."

He sighed. "That's a name I've had to live down. It sounds like somebody's Saint Bernard puppy!"

Lauren's eyes flew open and she began to laugh.

"What?" he demanded, a smile curving his mouth as he looked down at her and came to an unwilling halt.

Shaking her head, Lauren replied, "Nothing! You'll be embarrassed if I tell you, and—"

"Tell me. What's so funny?"

"It was my first impression, that's all." Lauren slid her hand up to his shoulder, holding him there lest her explanation offend him. "I thought you were somebody's big puppy that had gotten lost. You're very sweet, you know."

He looked at her askance, with doubt. "Are you sure? Not crazy?"

"No, you're not crazy. Just different. Fun different, though. Finn, I wish I knew you better!"

He smiled then, and bent closer. He kissed her lightly, gently, on the mouth. It was a quick kiss, and then he let her slide away from him, though he still held her hand, her fingers firmly caugh in his own. "Easy enough to fix. Let's go somewhere and listen to the music and talk."

"If we talk, we'll spoil the evening for everyone around us."

He smiled secretively and shook his head. He tugged her hand. "This way."

Curious, Lauren allowed him to lead her down the quay, perpendicular to the looming Aquarium building and away from the concert. The orchestra began again, this time playing a popular song, a theme from a recent movie. As their footsteps instinctively picked up the rhythm, Lauren swung his hand and asked, "Are you hijacking me again?"

"Not exactly. Here. Watch your step."

It was a boat. A sailboat, to be precise, moored nose and tail to the stout timbers of the quay. A lamp swung gently in the cabin, and a figure came out to meet them.

"Hi, Steve," Finn greeted him. "Everything okay?"

"Very quiet, boss," Steve reported. "Did you nab the dame?"

chapter 7

Lauren pulled back, startled.

"Don't listen to him," Finn said quickly. "He's only the hired help."

Steve looked affronted. "I suppose you want me to play the butler now? Drinks on the fantail?"

"Please," Finn agreed, helping Lauren step down into the boat. "Then you can disappear for an hour, all right?"

"Yes, sahib," Steve responded, bowing as he backed into the cabin of the sailboat. "My feet are like the wings of eagles, sahib."

"Don't mind him," Finn told Lauren. He pulled her along the deck until they reached the stern, where a pair of director's chairs stood side by side. Finn shunned them, however, and drew her to a built-in bench that had been covered with a plush cushion. There was room for two. "Steve is obnoxious to begin with, but he really gets cranky when I leave him alone for too long."

"Does he work full time for you?"

"Yep. He's my man Friday, I guess. Or my nursemaid.

Either way, I pay him a fortune to look after the details of my life."

Finn relaxed onto the cushion and tugged at Lauren's hand, but she stopped above him and turned to look around the luxurious boat. Her voice was full of admiration. "Finn, this is lovely! Is it yours?"

"Yes," he said. "I bought her three years ago."

The boat was long and sleek, perhaps an old racer that now served as Finn's pleasure boat. The deck was polished to a sheen, the cabin was built of a handsome teak, and the brass fittings shone with hard rubbing. The lamp in the cabin cast a golden glow on fine red leather upholstery. It was a big boat, and well taken care of. Lauren asked, "What's her name?"

"Frenchy," Finn said with a grin.

"Frenchy?" Lauren repeated, laughing. She sat beside him on the cushion. "That's not a name I can imagine you choosing."

"No?" He moved over just enough to give her some space beside him. "Remember *Destry Rides Again?* James Stewart played a sheriff who tries to run a corrupt town without using his guns."

"And Marlene Dietrich played the tough-but-heart-of-gold saloon singer."

"That's it." Finn nodded. "She was Frenchy. I love that movie."

"If I had to guess, I would have said your favorite movie was probably another Stewart film—*Harvey.*"

"The invisible rabbit? Do you think I'm that bizarre?" He laughed and quickly pleaded, "Don't answer that. *Harvey's* a close second to *Destry,* I'll admit. What else do you want to know?"

Lauren took a moment to study Finn, just as she had examined the boat a moment before. He was more relaxed now, more at ease with her. He met her eyes firmly, and his quick smile was not quite so shy. Boldly, she said, "I'd like to know everything."

"The whole Interface questionnaire?"

Lauren laughed and patted his arm. "No, I won't put you

through that ordeal. That takes hours to go through, you know! How did you make up all those questions?"

"I had help from experts," he said, taking her hand swiftly in his. "Hit me with the highlights, if you like."

"Okay." Lauren let him hold her hand and took a moment to organize her thoughts. She took a big breath. "Here goes, Mr. Gallagher. Born?"

"Syracuse, New York. Thirty-one years ago last April."

"Really? For some reason, I had a feeling you were a Californian."

"I went to school there," Finn explained, cocking his head to indicate he appreciated her intuition. "I got into college when I was fifteen, in fact, so—"

"Heavens! You are a genius, aren't you? Stanford?"

"Stanford, yes. Both my parents were tenured professors at Syracuse, but they moved to California when I went to school out there."

Lauren leaned back against the cushion, getting comfortable. "This is interesting. Didn't they trust fifteen-year-old Finnegan with all those California girls?"

He laughed. "I'm sure girls were the least of their worries. I was an extremely shy kid, believe it or not. So when—why are you laughing?"

"Nothing. Just the bit about you being shy. Tell me about your parents. How come they went to California with you?"

"They retired from teaching that year, that's all, and California seemed like a great place for them to go. They're still there, but getting—well—pretty old, I guess."

"What do you mean?" Lauren asked.

Finn explained, "I was their last child. I was kind of a fluke, you might say. My brother is forty-five and my sister is forty-two. I came along when my mother least expected to have another child. She was in her mid-forties when I was born."

"Good heavens!"

"Her words exactly."

Lauren laughed and held his hand. She felt suddenly as if the glow of the lamp extended as far as their comfortable spot on the bench, for she was toasty-warm beside him. It was nice to get to know somebody as totally honest as Finn. Her smile, she knew, reflected her sudden surge of warmth for him, for when Finn held her gaze, his own expression was alive with unspoken good feeling.

The moment stretched. There was nothing Lauren wanted more just then than for Finn to lean toward her, take her by the shoulders, and kiss her. Perhaps he saw the sudden desire in her face, because his touch on her hand changed, taking possession once more. He shifted and started to bend his head to hers.

"Hey, none of that while I'm still here," Steve interrupted as he came clomping out of the cabin. "Give me two minutes, and I'll be gone."

"Steve—" Finn began.

"Here. This is the best I could do. I didn't think you wanted me to make coffee or anything like that. Would you like me to open this?"

"This" was a magnum of champagne, a bottle that looked huge in the flickering lamplight.

"Wait a minute," Finn protested hastily. "There's got to be something else down there. Some soda, or something? I don't think we'd better—"

Steve rolled his eyes and said patiently, "This is what you drink in a situation like this, boss. Orange soda is not the ticket. Am I right, Doc?"

Lauren placed her hand on Finn's forearm and drew him back against her once more. "You're right, Steve. Honestly, Finn, champagne would be wonderful right now."

"Well, I wouldn't want you to think that I—" He cast around for the best way to phrase his anxiety and tried again. "If things got out of hand—or—well, I mean, if I didn't—"

"It's all right," Lauren soothed once more. "You're not going to get me drunk and take advantage of me, are you?"

Finn undoubtedly flushed, but the meagerness of the light prevented Lauren from being certain. Quickly, he said, "Of course not, Laurie. I'd never try—I mean—"

"Tough luck, Doc," Steve said conspiratorially as he brought forward a small table and set the two fluted glasses on it. He had a bucket for the bottle, as well. "Maybe you'll have to get the boss drunk and take advantage of him instead."

"See you later, Steve," Lauren said with a smile.

He saluted. "Right. Be back in an hour."

He leaped gracefully up onto the quay, and with his hands shoved down into the front pockets of his jeans, he went strolling in the direction of the lights and music. Lauren heard him start to whistle as soon as he was out of sight.

Finn opened the bottle, and the cork exploded off into the night. They heard it splash in the water just a few seconds later, a quiet little *kersploosh* that told them they were finally completely alone. They laughed softly together, and Finn poured the wine.

They talked then, hardly listening to the concert that continued behind them. At first Finn was the one who provided all the facts: The boat had been his first big purchase after the success of Interface, and he enjoyed spending time on it when he could get away from his computer.

"Tell me about your work," Lauren encouraged him. "You aren't spending all your time improving Interface, are you?"

"Not anymore," Finn agreed. "We did most of the tough stuff for Interface when I was still at Stanford."

"Really?" Lauren asked, surprised.

Finn smiled a little. "A friend and I started a match-up service in college. We were both several years younger than the other undergraduates, so we were social misfits. The girls treated us like a couple of cute mascots, and the guys ignored us until it was time to cram for exams. The computer was an easy way to make contact with the older crowd. We saw a need for getting men and women together on campus, and started to feed all the names and data into the program. We matched up a whole bunch of couples right away and made a—well, a campus splash, I suppose."

"Interface was born!"

"Sort of." Finn glanced at Lauren to be sure she was really interested in the story. Slowly, he continued, "After the first hundred names, we knew the system had to be

improved, so we tinkered around a while and finally had to
go see a psychiatrist who helped us with the first questionnaire. With his help, we refined the dating-service idea, and
the whole thing took off. We made a hundred thousand
dollars the second semester and started to franchise."

"How old were you?" Lauren demanded.

"Sixteen," Finn said.

"Good grief!"

"It was a fluke, I'll grant you," Finn began quickly, as
if apologizing. "We never intended to make such a bundle.
By the end of our three years at Stanford, we were both
rolling in money. Fortunately, we were too young to know
how to really blow it."

"Then what happened?" Lauren asked.

"Do you really want to know?" he asked doubtfully.

"Of course." Lauren sipped her champagne. "Where's
your friend now? Is he still working with you?"

Finn shook his head. "He sold most of his share of the
company to me about two years after we graduated. He
needed the cash for something else he wanted to try."

"What was that?"

Finn smiled. "Roger's a *real* genius. He's designing and
building computers in the Silicon Valley now. He did video
games for a while, and then started on home computers.
Now he does some systems for larger corporations. He's
got the right kind of stamina for that. It's a hellish business."

"What do you mean?"

Finn pretended to shudder. "I'd go crazy. The pressure
that gets generated around me is bad enough, but the com-
plexities of building—coordinating a thousand different
people and things and trying to market and service it all—
that's too overwhelming for me. Roger's doing okay, I
guess. I own an eighth of everything he owns, and he owns
an eighth of everything I do. The dividends he pays are a
lot higher than what I pay him."

"Why do you own a piece of each other?"

Finn shrugged happily. "We're not good at writing letters. This way we stay in touch."

Lauren laughed. "What else?"

"Oh," said Finn, going casual once more, "I help him out once in a while and he does me a favor now and then."

"Like what?" Lauren asked. "Just what do you do when you work, Finn Gallagher? Besides playing dating games?"

He refilled her glass very carefully. Unwillingly, he said, "My work is pretty boring most of the time."

"Quit stalling. What do you do?"

"I design software," Finn explained, and he looked at her. "Do you know what that means?"

"Sort of," Lauren said. "Software makes computers run. Without the programs, the computer is as useful as a—a—"

"A widget?" Finn suggested with a grin. "The machine won't function unless it's told what to do. I put the right commands together to make the computer useful for different purposes."

"Like what?"

He threw up his hands. "A thousand things! Why do you want to know all this?"

"It's interesting," Lauren insisted. "I'm a psychologist. I work in a totally different arena, and I wonder how you spend your time, that's all. Do you sell your own software designs, or what?"

"Sometimes," Finn said, giving in and answering her questions once more. "I put together a system for programming a certain line of home computers, and it's selling like crazy. Most of the time I do special jobs for big companies or organizations. I do a lot of consulting to government agencies. The Small Business Administration, the National Trust—even the FBI asks me for advice once in a while. Something different every week."

"Really?"

He nodded. "I try to take on projects that only last a week. That way I don't get bored or too nervous about deadlines and stuff. I can make my own rules now, and I'm trying to keep the pressure to a minimum. That part's no fun, and I want to enjoy my life."

Lauren smiled and touched his arm. "You seem to be succeeding."

"Not always," Finn corrected ruefully. "I've been busier lately than I intended."

"Why is that?"

He gave a small shrug. "I can't say no to somebody who needs help, I guess. Fortunately, *I* have help. I've hired a couple of guys to help me with the software."

"And Steve must be very useful."

"Yes," Finn agreed. "I put up with a lot of garbage from him, but I get a good deal of work accomplished in the car while Steve does the driving. He likes looking after me, no matter what he says."

Their conversation continued for a long time after that, and gradually Lauren began to supplement his stories with bits and pieces of her own life. He listened and laughed and asked her to elaborate, just as she had done with him. She found herself telling Finn about her family, about her job, and then about her friends. Gloria and Billy, mostly. She avoided telling Finn about her diverse collection of male friends, but he brought them up himself.

"You like people, don't you?" he asked when he had refilled their glasses again. "You work with them all day, and you play with your friends all night, it seems."

"Yes," Lauren agreed thoughtfully. "I do enjoy being out in the world. I don't spend much time alone, though I suppose I should more often."

"Why?"

"Because," she said slowly, thinking out her feelings as she spoke, "being alone would give me a better perspective on myself, right?"

Finn shrugged. "It mostly makes you lonesome."

That remark sparked Lauren's speculations. Very early in the conversation, she had begun to understand how a young man who had been raised practically as an only child by elderly parents, and later grew into an adolescent who excelled in computer science, could become, well, socially inept. Yes, the more she thought about it, Finn was probably a lonely fellow, even if he was a successful maverick in his computer business.

But Finn—perhaps seeing that he had confessed too much

too soon—changed the subject before Lauren could think
of a way to tactfully draw him out. They got off on another
conversational tangent. The time went quickly.

Finn was good company. He laughed and teased her,
then looked grave and shy when he thought he had over-
stepped the bounds of decorum. Lauren could see why he
was a scientist. He listened carefully, with real interest, and
showed such pleasure in each discovery that Lauren knew
he couldn't be pretending. He was sweet and thoughtful,
and tried hard to be sensible. Lauren enjoyed his refreshing
good humor, the gleam in his eyes, and the rollicking way
his laugh bubbled unexpectedly from inside him.

The strangest part of that hour, she decided much later,
was the way they couldn't keep their hands off each other.
She found herself reveling in the warmth of his thigh against
hers and the steady pressure with which he held her hand,
sometimes squeezing it between his two palms to emphasize
a point. Gradually, as the wine took effect, they loosened
up some more. Lauren bumped his shoulder with hers to
share her laughter. Finn brushed his fingertips along her
cheek, ostensibly to smooth her gently wisping hair. Finally,
he pulled her against his body, supposedly to keep her warm,
and as they talked, he traced a funny circular pattern on her
kneecap. In time, they were cuddling like lovers, heads
together, laughing.

Gradually, the talk wound down to nothing more than a
few syllables spoken softly in the darkness, and Finn got
very brave, indeed. Tugging gently but playfully at the hem
of her white dress, he said, "You know, you really look
wonderful tonight, Laurie."

"What?" Lauren asked in surprise, taken aback by his
sudden compliment.

He smiled shyly and kept his head down. "You took my
breath away when I first saw you at Harborplace."

"You were probably short of breath from performing all
those magic tricks while you waited for Philip and me to
come along." Lauren settled closer to him.

Finn laughed a little and touched the slightest of kisses
to her temple. "As soon as I saw you, I nearly bungled my

act. You're beautiful, you know. But tonight you're especially—you ought to have a parasol and a broad-brimmed hat to go with this dress. I love it."

"You and your costumes!"

He sat back in surprise. "I'm dressed quite conservatively!"

Lauren laughed and tugged at the bright-red tie that was still knotted at his collar. "Crimson cummerbund and suspenders to match, an exploding cane, and this—this thing doesn't light up, does it?"

Finn grabbed her up, still laughing, and said, "The only part of me that lights up, Doctor Chambers, is something that my cousin, a foolish Frenchman, would call a—"

Lauren got her fingertips to his mouth just in time to stop the words. "Don't tell me. You'll make me blush."

He smiled under her fingers, and his eyes were full of sparkling light. He dropped immediately into a terrible French accent. "I woode like to see ze *mademoiselle* blush, I tink."

Lauren's chest felt tight, and she could hardly breathe. With her mouth suddenly so close to his, she wanted nothing more than to be kissed. She smiled at his silly accent and murmured, "There's a nicer way to bring color to my life, you know, Maurice."

Finn was no fool, of course. And he didn't miss her invitation. He gathered Lauren up quite gently, smiling, and kissed her.

His mouth was firm and delicious, tasting crisply of champagne and teasing each of Lauren's senses just as subtly as the wine had done. She slipped her hands up his chest and parted her lips before she remembered herself. She mustn't scare him. She mustn't respond too eagerly. When Finn turned her body gently and pinned her against the railing, she was careful to swallow her murmur of delight.

He was more sure of himself this time, more eager, it seemed. He caught her head in one hand, running his fingers deeply into her hair to hold her securely to the kiss. He urged her mouth with a slight slanting of his own head and tasted her lips with his tongue. Lauren tried to hold back her sigh of response, but it escaped her trembling throat before she could smother the sound. Without thinking, she wound one arm around his shoulders. Instinctively, she pulled him down against her, all the while exploring the contours of his chest with her other hand. He was hard and smooth. Lauren slipped one of his suspenders off his shoulder, within the confines of his jacket. Finn laughed against her mouth at the sensation.

He broke the kiss, though gently, and for a long moment he gazed deeply into her eyes. Lauren felt him absorb a part of her in that time, as if he had memorized not only the shape of her face and the warmth of her eyes, but also some intangible quality. He took an unsteady breath and said, "You're a very kind woman, Lauren Chambers."

"Kind?"

He thought for a moment, struggling with a concept. "You—you're unique."

She smiled. "You said before that you didn't like the word *unique*."

His answering smile was rueful. "Only when people use it about me. You—you're something I didn't expect to find."

"Finn—"

His hand tightened gently on the nape of her neck to silence her. "I know. You don't have to say it. I've gone off the deep end over you, and it's a rash, immature thing to do. I feel like a sixth-grade kid in love with his teacher, so please—"

"Don't, Finn," Lauren said softly, stopping him. This was the first time he hadn't taken refuge in another character at a moment of intimacy, she noted. She was finding the *real* Finn Gallagher, the deeper, more honest Finn, infinitely more compelling than any of his created alter egos. For once this was his real voice talking, not a phony put-on, and Lauren hated stopping him when he was doing so well. But she said gently, "Don't put words in my mouth, all right? I think you're a darling, really. I enjoy being with you, despite the crazy ways you try to get my attention."

He ducked his head shyly, but didn't let her go. His hand drifted down the curve of her waist in a soft, caressing touch, but he was quiet, letting her speak.

"And I like being with you—like this—touching you, getting to know you." She lifted her fingertips to his cheek and caressed him lightly. "Don't be worried about me, all right? If you let nature take its course here, we just—well, there might be a very nice outcome."

His eyes snapped up to hers, filling with sparkle. "Laurie...?"

"I'm not in love with you," Lauren said quickly. "But I can see that it wouldn't be hard.... Finn, you're—well, you're adorable, and you shouldn't be so concerned about doing the right thing. I like you just the way you are. I hope I can see *all* the ways you are sometime."

"You don't mind too much that I snatched you away from Philip the Wonder Bore?"

"Yes, I do mind. Tomorrow I'm going to have to call Philip and apologize for both of us," Lauren said severely. "If you promise not to surprise poor Philip again, I'll tell you that no, I don't *really* mind that you snatched me away. I've enjoyed this time with you."

He bent and kissed her again, harder and with perceptible exuberance, before drawing back once more. "You're terrific. I can't believe I stumbled onto you. You really think I'm okay?"

"Of course I do."

"I'm not crazy?"

"Maybe a little," Lauren said with a laugh. "Don't push your luck, my friend."

He laughed and kissed her again quickly. He drew back, his eyes full of mischief, and his mouth curved into a quirky, boyish kind of smile that was hard to resist.

Lauren tugged at his tie. "Come back here."

Finn obeyed, returning to kiss her again, his hand resting on the flare of her hip this time. Perhaps he wasn't aware of the way he touched her there, but as his kiss deepened, Lauren abruptly thought her dress must be scorched by the contact of his hand. Again she felt the tingling rush of pleasure as he kissed her, the warm tide of emotion as he handled her so considerately.

As he found her mouth and savored its shape more thoroughly this time, Lauren's mind began to cloud with new sensations. How might this gentle man make love to her? How might his tentative touch on her hip change if she gave him some sign of assent? Would he turn bold and undress her? Smooth her skin beneath quick, exploring hands? Or might he need to be encouraged and instructed? Would she have to tell him what she wanted and enjoyed? Suddenly breathless with the images that filled her imagination, Lauren tore her mouth from Finn's, eyes closed, and took a breath of air to clear her head.

Finn stayed close, breathed her name very softly, and began to explore the length of her throat. His mouth was soft, giving her gentle, open-mouthed nibbles, and then he seemed to inhale deeply of the scent that clung to her skin. He kissed her throat, seeking her pulse with his lips. He slipped his hand down her hip, down to the curving muscle of her thigh, and Lauren felt a fresh surge of heated awareness overwhelm her.

He was an expert, whether he knew it or not. She was practically trembling with desire, and he had barely touched her! By now, a braver man might have her dress unbuttoned and be fondling the bare skin beneath, but not Finn. He laid his hands on her gently, sweetly, and let her passions seethe.

Lauren found herself losing control. Like a sex-starved teenager, she ran her hands all over his chest, over his shoulders, unsteadily sliding the jacket from his back. His suspenders made an unyielding Y on his back, but underneath, his flesh was wonderfully masculine and firm. His shirt tucked neatly into the back of his trousers but did not obscure the hard curve of his lower back and the neat flex of his hips and thighs. She heard herself whisper his name unsteadily. There was nothing cool and sedate about Dr. Lauren Chambers now. She was steaming inside, as if a savory potion of desire had been heated to a delicious simmer.

Finn took her mouth again with his, but he was smiling. He kissed her hard, once, twice, three times. "Laurie. Laurie, you're so warm, so easy to touch. I want to take my time with you, but I can't—it's very hard not to forget myself with you."

So forget yourself, please! Lauren wanted to scream. Stop teasing me like this!

Slowly, he smoothed his hand up the curve of her waist, past the soft leather belt to the quaking rise of her abdomen. Just above his fingers, her breasts were aching for his touch. He said, "Let me, please? I'd like to feel your heartbeat, Laurie."

"Yes," she whispered, hardly able to keep from seizing his hand and crushing him to the heat of her breast.

He moved then, with agonizing slowness. His fingertips eased higher, higher until he met the delicate weight of her breast. He stopped too soon, though, and probed deeply into her soft skin. He must have found her swift pulse there below her breast, for he took a long breath of relief and kissed her throat, her neck, her mouth.

Lauren opened her lips and melted to him, her tongue seeking to make contact with his. Then she explored the contours of his mouth, savoring the taste and shape with growing impatience. Had he no idea how she felt? It was as if a boiling pot of bubbling passion had been overturned inside her and was now running like hot oil through her body. She was quivering! Her thighs felt so hot she could hardly keep her knees locked together—all because he wouldn't give in and touch her breast! Why didn't he find her nipple with his palm and just—oh, please, Finn! Was there a bed in that cabin just a few feet away?

Then he did it. He inched up just enough and cupped her breast, laying his thumb ever so gently against her painfully erect nipple. How could he not feel the urgent little thrust through her whispery-soft dress? How could he not guess from her half-panting breath and careening heartbeat that she was teetering on the brink of sensual explosion? In fact, Lauren realized with dawning shock, the inexorable spiral of sensations was getting so out of hand that she was actually approaching a kind of mini-climax. If he squeezed

her breast, she was going to do something she'd never done
in her entire life—reach an ecstatic plane in a man's arms
while both of them were completely dressed!

Abruptly, she twisted out of Finn's kiss, confused and
very embarrassed. Worse, frightened out of her wits. How
could the man affect her this way?

"I'm sorry," Finn said immediately. "I shouldn't have
touched you like that. I had no right. Please forgive me,
Lauren. I'm terribly sorry."

Lauren stared at him as he blushed and fumbled his way
through half a dozen apologies. Didn't he understand? Did
he really think he had behaved badly? The man was more
than unique! He was matchless, peerless, timeless! Blankly,
Lauren watched him stumble and try to collect his composure. He did not release her, though, and for that she was
glad. She lay in his arms and began to smile. The smile
turned to a grin, and the grin to a giggle. Lauren began to
laugh hysterically.

"What's wrong?" Finn asked anxiously. "Please—"

"Nothing's wrong," Lauren finally managed to say. "Finn,
you're the sweetest man on earth! Where have you been all
my life?"

Finn was stunned into bewildered silence by that dec-
laration, and he watched Lauren giggle for a long moment.
He might have figured out an appropriate response in that
time, but he was saved from having to say something by
the timely return of Steve.

As Steve clambered down onto the deck, Finn pulled his
arm from around Lauren, and with a last, puzzled look down
at her, he turned his attention to his returning employee.

"The concert's over," Steve reported. "I think it's time
to set sail for the doc's house."

"Yes, please," said Lauren, wiping the tears of bemused
hilarity from her eyes. "I think I'd better go home before I
really embarrass myself."

There was no car, of course, so the only solution was
to take the boat out into the river and to Lauren's condominium. Steve revved up the boat's powerful engine, then

dashed to cast off the lines. Finn left her to help maneuver the boat, and Lauren sat in quiet enjoyment in the stern, watching him.

He *was* unique, no doubt about it. Working with the boat, he looked as handsome as any of Errol Flynn's recent imitators. He was a charmer, all right. In his fancy trousers and handsome white shirt, he looked dashingly attractive in the moonlight. The crimson Y of his suspenders only seemed to exaggerate the width of his shoulders and the narrowness of his lean waist. Yes, a very attractive charmer was Finnegan T. Gallagher.

Though she had some experience with boats herself, Lauren remained in the background and let the men work. They functioned well together, evidence that they had been teammates for some time. Finn was clearly an expert yachtsman and the boss, Lauren noted. When he called an order to check the depth of the water, Steve scrambled to obey.

With great care, Finn guided the handsome sailboat close to the shore. The lights of the grouped condominiums shone up on the bank, and Steve carefully poled the boat as close as was safe.

Finn threw an anchor overboard with a great splash and came striding back to Lauren.

"All set, I think."

"I'm hardly dressed for swimming," Lauren countered cheerfully. "I don't suppose you've got a spare bikini?"

A twinkle appeared in his eyes. "Now that you mention it, a spare bikini might be a great addition to our regular gear."

"Hmm. I'm supposed to do some skinny-dipping, is that it?"

"No, no," Finn assured her, taking her arm. "This way, milady. Your longboat awaits."

Steve had dragged what appeared to be a deflated rubber dinghy from inside the cabin, and with a terrific yank, he set off the self-inflating tank. Lauren squealed at the noise, and then started laughing. The dinghy came alive, opening and growing larger and larger every second.

Finn sidestepped the thing warily and said, "I'll set you ashore myself. The only thing is, I can't guarantee that you won't get a little wet. I've got some spare clothing in the cabin, if you'd like to take your dress off first. I'd hate for you to spoil it."

"Are you looking for an excuse to get me out of my clothes?" Lauren asked, before she thought.

Finn blushed and stammered, and Lauren had to joke him out of being embarrassed. In the end, she did change into a big pullover sweater of his, and with her dress rolled up into a bundle and pressed into a plastic bag, she went down into the dinghy with him.

Splashing each other and giggling like kids, they paddled the unsteady vessel to the shore, and Lauren hopped out into knee-deep water. "No, no," she told Finn, holding him down into the bobbing dinghy with one hand and trying to keep her bundle of clothing above the water with the other. "You'll ruin your trousers. Good night, Finn. Thank you. I had a wonderful evening."

Finn caught her wrist. "You're not just saying that?"

Lauren leaned close and kissed him on the mouth. She smiled into his eyes. "No, I'm not. Drive carefully, will you? The freeway to Washington is murder this time of night."

"I think we'll stop a lot of traffic with the boat, don't you?"

Lauren smiled. "Will you call me again?"

"As soon as I can," Finn promised, letting go reluctantly. "I wish you were coming with me."

"Some day soon I'll ask you to come with me, but..." Lauren hesitated a moment, and finally decided to be sensible. "Not tonight."

"No," Finn agreed softly.

"Finn," Lauren began before she could stop herself. "Once before you told me..."

"Yes?"

Lauren squeezed her eyes closed. "Thatyouwantedto-makelovetome," she breathed, running the words together quickly.

"Yes," Finn said quietly.

She swallowed. Did he have to make this so awfully hard? Trying to master her voice, Lauren asked, "Do you—? I mean, am I still . . . ?"

"I don't want to rush anything," Finn said gently, and he touched her face lightly with his fingertips. He tipped her face to his and waited until Lauren cautiously opened her eyes before he brushed her mouth with a kiss. Then he said, "I—we've both got a lot to think about first, Laurie. I'll call you soon, all right?"

chapter 8

BUT FINN DID not call. Two days went by, and then two more, and the man did not phone! Lauren racked her brain for a reason, but couldn't come close to fathoming why.

He had said they both had some thinking to do. The more she fumed about his not calling, the more Lauren began to review every word Finn had said that night on his boat. What had he meant by "We both have a lot to think about"? Was he having second thoughts? *Now?*

By Thursday, Lauren threw aside all her old-fashioned scruples about women calling men and tried the phone number on his business card.

Curses! He had an answering machine.

"Hi," said his recorded voice, sounding truly apologetic. Amazing, Lauren thought, what a man's voice can do to a lady's baser instincts when she least expects it. One syllable from him, and her brain turned off completely. Her stomach plunged to a location somewhere between her knees and ecstasy, and she had to sit down quickly. Unaware of the effects of his gentle tone on the listening audience, the recorded Finn continued with sincere regret, "I'm sorry I can't answer your call right now. If you leave your name and number, I'll be sure to call you back as soon as I can."

Lauren was silent even after the beep sounded. What to say to a man you had decided to lust after?

The final beep sounded before she could formulate a sensible message, even in her own mind. Five minutes later, she called back. "Finn," she said to the tape machine, "it's Lauren Chambers. Remember me? Your fellow champagne drinker with the wet feet? Am I going to hear from you sometime? Call me when you can, please."

And then Lauren waited another two days. Finn still did not call, and she was darned if she was going to plead with an answering machine. What had happened? Had she insulted him? Frightened him? Shocked him? Disappointed him? What? Why didn't he *call?*

On Saturday, she got into her car and drove to Washington. After all, every American ought to visit the nation's capitol now and then, right? Lauren grinned wryly to herself. No use trying to justify what you're doing, Doctor Chambers, she rebuked herself. Admit it. You've fallen for this guy.

She drove to Washington and wondered what she was going to say to Finnegan T. Gallagher when—if?—she caught up with him.

It was afternoon before Lauren got the courage to start driving along the Georgetown street in search of Finn's address. And after she had found the house, she sat for a long time in her car before she was brave enough to go to the door. After all, how would a bashful fellow like Finn react to a pursuing woman?

The building was a very large and imposing Federal-style house located on a once elegant treelined street several blocks from Embassy Row. The homes on both sides were big and pretty, but crumbling just a bit. The sidewalk was cracked, with tufts of grass growing up through the concrete, and the cars parked under the trees were vintage models, not the extremely expensive luxury cars that typified more affluent sections of Georgetown. It was the sort of neighborhood that Lauren recognized as being filled with graduate students, or perhaps newly married professionals, a few retired government employees, or young singles who shunned spanking-clean—and therefore characterless—condominiums. Looking up, Lauren noted that some of the windows in Finn's house had been thrown open to the early-June sunshine.

She moved to knock, but the front door was standing half-open. Cautiously, Lauren tipped the leaded-glass door wide before she ventured to poke her head inside. "Finn?"

No response. Lauren noted a wall of mailboxes, and she realized that the house was an apartment building. That might explain the open door. She read the names on the boxes and found GALLAGHER 3A.

She walked to the huge, curving walnut stairway and started up. The steps had been swept, but they creaked as she set foot on each one. Someone's stereo was thumping an oldie-but-goodie Rolling Stones number from above, and it added to the cacophony of other thin-walled-apartment noises. A sweet odor of baking hung in a cloud around the first landing, and Lauren could hear the tinny music of a television there also. One door was standing open, and at the sound of Lauren's footsteps someone came to the door and pulled it wider.

Lauren hesitated, for she had come face to face with a young woman. She was thin and rather wild-haired, and she didn't speak when she saw Lauren. The woman's eyes were clear and blue and full of apprehension.

"Hi," Lauren said cheerfully. "I'm looking for Finnegan Gallagher."

The young woman didn't answer. She closed the door.

Hmm. Finn's neighbors weren't exactly the friendly type. With a shrug, Lauren walked around the newel post and went up the next flight, toward Mick Jagger's shouting voice.

There was only one door on the third floor, and it, too, was standing open. The music was deafening there. Lauren called, "Finn?", then raised her voice and shouted, "Finn!"

He was at home, for he responded from somewhere, "Back here, Betsy!"

Betsy? Emboldened, Lauren stepped into his apartment.

She had expected the unusual, perhaps even the bizarre, but an accurate description of Finn's apartment went even beyond such terms. Lauren looked around with amazement, and then growing interest. This was truly a curiosity shop.

The furniture ranged in type from a sedate Shaker-style table and bow-backed Windsor chairs to a sofa—at least Lauren assumed Finn used it as a sofa, for it was an enormous piece of furniture created in the shape of a huge pink human hand complete with crimson fingernails. Lauren smiled at the thought of Finn relaxing there with his long legs dangling over the thumb.

An orange crate served as an end table, and an elegant glass-and-brass sculpture stood at the other end of the peculiar sofa. The windows were open wide, and the resulting breeze stirred a beautiful wicker birdcage that hung from the ceiling. There was no living bird inside, just a pair of handmade toy doves locked together in a winged embrace with sleepy, slightly foolish smiles sewn into their beaks. On an antique buffet of indeterminate age, Lauren discovered three small wire cages lined up and connected by a series of oversized gerbil tunnels. There were two snoozing rabbits inside, one black and one spotted; both adorable. For the magic tricks, no doubt.

The walls of the airy apartment were cluttered with all manner of memorabilia, including an oar, the head of a rhinoceros—fake, of course—with a silly grin on its face, a framed picture of George Washington that looked just like the one that had hung in the principal's office of Lauren's elementary school, and a huge yellow highway sign that read NO STOPPING. Stuffed toys were piled on the hundreds of paperback books cluttering a set of shelves that had been built out of two stepladders and a series of planks. A black silk top hat hung rakishly on the antenna of a small portable television.

The Rolling Stones were blasting from an elaborate reel-to-reel tape system, and when the last notes of the song died away, Lauren quickly crossed to the machine and switched it off. The resulting silence was a blessing.

"Betsy?" Finn called again.

Lauren followed his voice back through the hallway. She passed a large, pink-tiled bathroom and a monastically bare bedroom that contained no more than a maple dresser, a rumpled double bed and a pretty white Indian rug. There was another door at the end of the hall, and Lauren peeked cautiously through it.

This was where Finn worked. It was as large as the living room but packed from floor to ceiling with what seemed to be computer equipment. Screens and keyboards and bright-blue cables appeared to link one machine to the next in a tangled chain of winking, beeping gadgetry. A printer tapped furiously under a clear plastic hood, feeding green and white striped paper into a wire basket.

Finn was there, of course, sitting in a functionally comfortable steno-type chair with his sneakers propped on an unplugged disc drive. There were half a dozen empty cola cans lined up on the desk at his elbow. The green computer screen before him flashed a column of figures, rhythmically ticking upward like movie credits. Finn didn't take his eyes from the busy screen. Without turning around, he said absently, "Hi."

Clearly, he hadn't shaved in several days. His hair was even curlier and more unruly than before. He was dressed in a simple lemon-colored T-shirt with VASSAR lettered on the front and a fawn-soft pair of blue jeans that must have dated from the last decade. He was concentrating, working hard, and Lauren was suddenly sorry she had come. She knew she shouldn't be interrupting.

"Everything okay?" Finn asked, still reading the screen.

Well, she couldn't very well turn around and leave without saying something. Lauren tiptoed into the component-cluttered room and gave Finn a quick kiss on the top of his head. "Hi."

He jabbed a button on the keyboard and spun around in surprise. "Lauren!"

"I'm sorry to come barging in like this. I didn't mean to interrupt . . ."

He didn't get out of his chair but caught her hips in his hands, immediately pulling her close. In spite of his scruffy appearance, his eyes were full of delighted sparkle and his mouth curved in genuine pleasure as he looked up at her. "What are you doing here?" he demanded in amazement. "I didn't think—are you—Oh, Lord!" He clapped one hand to his forehead. "I was supposed to call you, wasn't I?"

Laughing at his delight, his confusion, and then his dismay, Lauren said swiftly, "Don't worry about it. When I didn't hear from you, I got concerned, that's all. I really don't want to interrupt, Finn. You're busy, and I can—"

"Don't go yet. I'm surprised that you're here. Astonished, even. How did you find this place?"

"I still have your business card," Lauren said simply. "I keep it with the paper flower you gave me."

He smiled and his firm grasp on Lauren's hips turned gentle; it was almost a caress. He didn't let her go, but pulled her more securely between his knees. Tipped up to hers, his face looked very young beneath a few days' growth of dark beard. He said, "I've missed you. I've thought about you, honestly. I should have called. I'm sorry. I've been . . ." He made a helpless gesture at the computers around him, and gave a shrug. "I've been working. I'm sorry."

"Don't apologize. I shouldn't have dropped in."

"I can't spend time with you even now," he went on, his eyes filling with dismay once more. "I've got to stay and finish this—"

"I can see you're busy," Lauren said, and she touched his face to soothe him. His beard was prickly beneath her fingers, and she smiled at the sensation. "I should say I'm sorry and go."

Finn was reluctant to agree with her, but the computer behind him gave a warning beep, and he couldn't stop an anxious glance at the machine. He said quickly, "I promise I'll call you. I'll be done by tonight, I'm sure. I'll come get you tomorrow, all right? We'll go out on the boat if the weather's nice. Is the weather nice?"

"Goodness, how long have you been cooped up in this room?" Lauren asked with a laugh. "It's been lovely outside. Yes, tomorrow would be nice. Go back to work now, before that thing blows a gasket."

"Lauren," Finn began urgently, his hands tightening on her hips.

He was too shy to ask, so Lauren interpreted the expression in his eyes for herself and bent to kiss him.

His mouth was quick to find hers and tasted wonderfully masculine. His cheek was rough against her chin, but Lauren reveled in the exciting contact. She wanted more immediately. She slipped her hand down to the back of his neck and laid the fingertips of her other hand along his cheek, then parted her lips and swept her tongue along his mouth, teasing him.

Finn sighed, slid his hand up her side to her back, and pulled. In a moment, he had Lauren neatly in his lap, and he wound both arms around her body, pulling her tightly, sensually, against his chest. He deepened the kiss and met her tongue with his, delving swiftly into her mouth this time. No uncertainty, no hesitation, just instantaneous, roiling sexual power.

Lauren slipped her arms around Finn's shoulders and gave in peacefully. Excitement tingled in her stomach. Yes, this was what she wanted. She had dreamed of this moment for days. Finn's body was taut and hard against hers. His mouth was sweet, and his hands moved hungrily up the curve of her back. She felt the surge of strength in his arms and wondered for the briefest instant if Finn was going to pick her up and carry her. His bedroom lay just a few yards down the hall, and with the late-spring breeze and glorious sunshine pouring through the windows, what better time and place to discover a much-longed-for intimacy?

But, no. The printer quit tapping and suddenly began to shriek like a wounded alien from a faraway planet, and the computer terminal gave a last warning noise and began to spew out more numbers. Finn jerked under her and began to laugh.

Lauren wanted to shout with frustration.

"I'm sorry," Finn said, easing her off his lap. "This just can't wait, Laurie."

Tapping her foot with annoyance, she watched as he scooted his chair across the floor and lifted the lid on the printer. He shut off the alarm, unsnapped the carriage, and popped out a ribbon cartridge. As he replaced the ribbon, he said over his shoulder, "I'll understand if you give up on me, you know. This must seem awfully silly to you. Have you apologized to Philip Whatsisname for Saturday night yet?"

"Yes, I prostrated myself."

"Did you go out with him, too?"

"Would you be angry if I did?" Lauren asked, not thinking straight as she collected herself from his kiss.

Finn set the ribbon into the printer and closed the lid before turning back to her. With his eyes serious and his voice gone soft, he said, "Not angry, no. Sad, though."

Oh, curse him! Looking like a lost spaniel again! Lauren's annoyance melted away and she couldn't stop her smile. She sighed and said, "No, I didn't go out with Philip."

Finnegan Gallagher grinned and zipped his chair back to the terminal again. "I'm glad. I'll call, okay? I promise."

It was a dismissal, of course, and Lauren felt suddenly foolish and awkward. Finn caught up with the numbers on the terminal and quickly typed in some data. Lauren faded to the doorway, watching for a moment as he worked before she turned and walked slowly back down the hall. When she passed his bedroom, she averted her eyes and ground her teeth.

So this was what it was like. How many times had she fended off a man's sexual advances because of the absence of the commitment she needed? How many times had she sent a man away from her door feeling exactly as she did now? How did men stand this awful, empty longing?

She closed Finn's apartment door firmly and started down the steps, steadying herself on the bannister. Her legs were weak and quivery, and she didn't want to risk a tumble and have Finn find her days later on the landing. She'd probably be feverishly muttering his name and try to tear his shirt off! For the first time in her life, Lauren understood the purpose of a cold shower.

On the second floor, she was surprised to find the blond woman waiting at her half-opened door. Lauren smiled, and this time the woman came out on the landing. She had a china tureen in her hands.

"Hello, again," Lauren said, preparing to go down the steps.

The blonde cleared her throat nervously and inquired, "Are you taking care of him today?"

Lauren hesitated. "Taking care of Finn?"

The blonde nodded quickly. "I made some soup for his supper, but if you're going to look after him . . ."

Lauren shook her head slowly, thinking. "No, I'm not bringing him any food. I just stopped by to say hello."

"Oh."

As a trained psychologist, Lauren recognized a certain dullness in the woman's eyes, a slight hesitancy in her speech, and the uncertain way she stood in the doorway. Lauren had seen this kind of woman many times before. Either she had been abused as a child, or had been through some drug or alcohol problem, or had spent time in a mental institution. There were any number of possibilities, but Lauren knew this woman's mental health was not at its best. The blonde stared at Lauren like a startled forest animal.

This was a halfway house, Lauren suddenly guessed. A home for people who were easing back into the normal world. To put the other woman at ease, she smiled and said, "Finn is upstairs now, if you'd like to see him. He's working at the moment, but—"

"Here," said the woman, abruptly thrusting the tureen into Lauren's hands. "You take it up to him. I—I don't like to bother him when he's busy."

Lauren smiled kindly. "I'm sure he'd like to see you— to thank you for the food, at least."

The blonde shook her head quickly, retreating into the apartment. "You take it. I'll see him sometime."

"Wait," Lauren called as the door began to close. "Are you—is your name Betsy, by any chance?"

"No," said the woman. And she closed the door.

Hmm. Lauren stood there for a long minute, holding the hot soup dish and wondering. Exactly what did all this mean? Here was rich and renowned Finn Gallagher living in a less-than-posh house with heaven knew how many young women who doted on him so much that they made his meals for him. And who the hell was Betsy, anyway?

Lauren made a U-turn and started back up the steps. There was no way she could endure the drive back to Baltimore without knowing a few answers first. She'd camp out in Finn's living room until he had time to eat his soup and talk.

chapter 9

AFTER PUTTING THE soup in Finn's refrigerator, Lauren spent a few minutes cleaning up the kitchen. In the sink were a few dishes that had been rinsed but not washed, so she cleaned and dried them and found their places in Finn's extraordinarily neat shelves. She wondered if perhaps other women had cooled their heels in this kitchen and had found such chores to keep themselves busy while awaiting Finn's attentions.

The hours might have passed very slowly if Lauren's mind hadn't been filling full of more and more questions about the unique Mr. Gallagher.

She waited until the sun went down, listening to Finn talk on the telephone or typing on the computer. She nibbled on a piece of cheese at six, then kicked off her shoes and lay down on the giant palm of the sofa to wait. Eventually, she fell asleep...

"Hey."

"Yes," Lauren murmured in answer. "Yes, please, Finn."

He jiggled her shoulder again and blew a soft breath into her ear just before he kissed her temple. "Laurie, you're going to get a terrible crick in your neck if you sleep here much longer."

"Wha—?" Lauren woke then, coming out of her dream like a rocket out through a cloud bank. The room was dark except for a light that spilled from the bathroom, and Finn was crouched beside the sofa, inches away. She sat up quickly. "Finn!"

"Gosh," he said, rocking back on his heels. "I didn't mean to scare you."

He must have been in the shower, for he smelled pleasantly of soap and his hair was still damp at the ends. He hadn't shaved, though, and for one heart-stopping moment, Lauren thought he was naked. But, no, he had put on a pair of pajama trousers before coming out to find her asleep on his sofa. Without his shirt, his shoulders looked wonderfully golden and tantalizingly touchable. Lauren hugged her elbows to stop herself from reaching out to caress him.

Finn placed his hand on Lauren's knee to calm her and said, "I didn't know you were still here. I thought you left hours ago."

"I did," Lauren said, shivering under his hand. Her voice was whispery from sleep, but she added, "I came back, though. Finn, who's Betsy?"

He smiled into her eyes, his own dark irises full of warmth and amusement. "Are you awake yet?"

"Awake enough, yes."

Finn put his fingers to Lauren's temple and slipped her dark hair back from her face. He caressed her long, loose hair and explained with a smile, "Betsy lives downstairs in one-B. She looks in on me sometimes. Did you meet her?"

"No." Lauren shook her head. "Do you sleep with her?"

Finn's eyes popped open in surprise, and he laughed. "What's this all about? Of course not!"

"Do you sleep with anybody?"

He cocked his head and watched her eyes, a smile coming and going on his mouth as if he couldn't quite figure out what she was leading up to. Evidently, words failed him.

Lauren put her hands to his bare chest in a tentative touch. She asked again, "Do you, Finn?"

He apparently decided to go for honesty. "Lately? No, I haven't been sleeping with anyone, Lauren. Have you?"

"No," Lauren said steadily, in spite of the crazy way her heart and lungs seemed to be functioning. Unable to meet his direct and uncomplicated gaze, she said, "I haven't. I'm not a one-night stand, Finn."

"I never thought you were."

"Thank you," Lauren said, swallowing hard. "But, Finn, there are times when people—even people who are very strict with themselves, like me—want to—to make love with someone before—well, before they really know each other well enough."

"I see," he said gravely.

Maybe she had awakened too fast, or maybe it was just the quiet way he waited for the truth to come out, but Lauren stumbled ahead, saying, "I—well, it's very out of character for me, and I don't want you to think that this is something I do regularly, because what's happening here is—is quite extraordinary for me, but I—I just—well, I—"

He touched her chin, lifting her face to the light. He had a Cheshire Cat's grin on his mouth, and he asked, "Lauren Chambers, are you stuttering?"

"Oh, curses, Finn Gallagher!" Lauren whispered, squeezing her eyes tight shut.

He tipped her head a fraction higher and touched his lips very, very softly to hers. Then, with a wicked grin, he fell into a throaty French accent. "Ah, *chérie*, you save me from ze worst embarrassment. I would stutter even more zan you."

Lauren slipped her arms around his neck, a giggle starting. "Oh, Finn."

"At least you do not take me for my French cousin," Finn cracked, pulling Lauren up from the depths of humiliation with yet another of his silly routines. He kissed her temple then, and her cheekbone, and finally her lips. "My cousin would say, 'Let me take you to zee Casbah, my sweet *pomme frite*.' But I—I am not such a Casanova." He abandoned the French accent abruptly and said, "Lauren. Can we? Should we?"

Lauren opened her eyes and smiled. "Make love? Oh, yes, please, Finn."

He held her in his arms then, cradling her body gently before him. He let out a long, uneven breath and murmured softly in his own voice, "I thought we'd never get to this point."

Surely, he wasn't going to go shy on her again. Not now, of all moments. Was she going to have to take command of even this situation? With trembling hands, Lauren slid a caress down Finn's arms until her palms rested on his wrists. With an encouraging squeeze there, she began coaxingly, "Finn..."

"Not here," he said, and there came the lightest sliver of a laugh. "I'd feel as if King Kong were going to snatch us up any minute. Come, Laurie."

He pulled her up out of the lumpy palm of the sofa and took her hand in his. He was very tall above her for a split second, hesitating as if giving her a last chance to refuse. But Lauren was quiet, and so Finn turned. He led her to the hall, past the bath, and into his bedroom. He left the door open so that the light cast a soft illumination as far as the bed. He pulled her behind him to the window, which he left open, but he released a thick curtain, and suddenly the room was a secluded niche, intimate and quiet, high above the street and the rest of the world.

He turned back to her, pulling her quivering body close. Into the tumbled hair above her ear, he said very softly, "Now..."

Whatever concerns Lauren had about their respective roles in this seduction were allayed within the next thirty seconds. Finn cupped her head and delivered one of the most sizzling kisses imaginable, and then began to purposefully unfasten the buttons of her blouse. He found her throat with his mouth, and as he descended the line of buttons, he kissed her time and again, lower and lower, until the wispy barrier of her bra prevented his further descent. He peeled her shirt off unceremoniously, ignoring

her instinctive gasp, and laid it on the dresser. With one
hand, he unclasped her bra with a maneuver that must have
been well practiced. In another moment, Lauren was bare-
breasted and breathless.

He gathered her up then, holding her body against his
chest to feel the rounded softness of her breasts pressed
against him, and just as quickly he kissed her mouth. He
tasted fleetingly of peppermint toothpaste, but the flavor
quickly evaporated as the kiss grew in fervency. His mouth
was firm and sure as he took command of hers.

Delighted, Lauren wound her arms high around his neck
and aligned her body with his lean frame. She molded her
lips to his, obeying when he eased her mouth farther open
to better savor the swift current of sexual release. He passed
his hands down her back, smoothing her flesh beneath his
firm palms, and she found herself writhing like a cat under
soft caresses.

He pressed kiss after melting kiss to the thumping pulse
in Lauren's throat, then brought his fingers up to brush her
hair back from the nape of her neck. He seemed to breathe
deeply of some mysterious scent there, and then he murmured in a husky voice, "Lauren, darling, stop me if I go
too fast. I can't—I want you so badly."

Somehow, they were on the bed, and Finn placed her
head on the pillow. He held Lauren's eyes firmly, then
quickly, carefully, finished undressing her. He took one of
her long, bare legs in hand, admiring its slender strength
with a caress, and gently curled it around his own hip so
that they were locked together. Above her, he began to
stroke her body, learning each curve, each rib. Perhaps he
could not select a character from the repertoire in his limitless
imagination who might best make love to her, so he was
silent. He bent to kiss her mouth, then her throat, and from
the reverent way he pressed his lips first here, then there,
Lauren knew he found her beautiful.

She smiled tremulously and drew gentle patterns on his
chest before she ventured further. Lauren enjoyed Finn's
exploration. He slid his sensitive fingers over her skin and
bent to trace the same path with his lips. She closed her

eyes to take pleasure in the gently sensual moment, and Finn kissed her breast. He licked her there, and suddenly took her in his mouth. Lauren gasped, but held his head still, lacing her fingers in his dark hair. He was quick and sharp, and the sudden roughness was delicious. Lauren felt as if Finn was draining her inhibitions with that inexorable suction and the not-too-gentle tug of his teeth—all clues of pleasures to come. She released her own sigh of affirmation.

He was impatient for her touch, she supposed, and when she slid her own hands lower and rested them on his hip-bones, he couldn't stop a small shudder of anticipation. Matching his quickness, she eased inside the cotton waist-band and with his help drew off the last garment that remained between them. His skin was smooth and warm to her touch. When he settled firmly against her reclining slimness, Lauren found the lean power of his body suddenly sparking a very real need within herself—the need to know Finn, to experience him, and soon. She gathered him close and longed to whisper words of encouragement.

Finn was no innocent boy in need of teaching, however. He was quick and strong and uninhibited.

He pinned her wrists together, and then teased her body with an expert's touch that wasted no time. He caressed, then explored and purposefully sought her sensitive flesh before touching so sweetly, so swiftly again. He was too fast, and yet not fast enough, it seemed. Lauren lay beneath him and alternately cried "Yes," or "Wait!" until she had to laugh breathlessly at her own mindless responses. Never had her own voice sounded so husky, so demanding. Finn was quiet, watching her eyes and smiling, or swooping to kiss her with a quickness that repeatedly sent her senses spiraling downward into a delicious chasm.

At last he allowed Lauren her freedom, and she touched him everywhere, enjoying the taut muscle at the curve of his back, the neat joining of his hip and thigh. She found him, caressed him, and enjoyed the startled excitement he displayed as she fondled his lean length and cupped him like warm embers in her hands. She laughed in delight, and Finn caught her head between his hands and kissed her hard.

In the next moment, they were wrestling, rolling this way and that on the crisp cotton sheets and exuberantly touching, learning, taking pleasure.

And then Finn trapped Lauren on her back, and with a pounding heart she wrapped her thighs around his lithe hips to hold him still above her. He pinned her shoulders hard into the bed, and at his unarguable strength, Lauren convulsively tightened her slim legs and murmured his name. With one hand slid firmly under the small of her back, Finn arched her body to meet him. He took her swiftly and gave a small growl in his throat when he sank within her. Lauren cried out involuntarily at the quick heat, but Finn pressed further, until they were deeply coupled and gasping together.

He was gentler then, satisfied for the moment by the long-awaited quenching of their mutual thirst for each other. Finn was still, and Lauren remained quiet for a moment, a smile curving her lips. Finn touched them with a kiss. Lauren's throat tightened with emotion. He was a darling, a gentle, naive boy with the deep-running passion of a man. She drew him down to her until they were one body, locked and melded. He was a lover, yes . . . oh, yes.

The lull of recognition did not last, and Lauren could feel the urgency building within herself once more. She could feel the quickening of Finn's heart and the steady increase of his respiration—a tempo that she unconsciously matched with her own. The longed-for moment quickly slid by. She wanted more, and she knew Finn was suddenly just as hungry for release.

Together they began to move . . . first softly, then with growing passion. The swift joining and withdrawal gathered speed. The rhythm turned more urgent, more violent with each passing heartbeat, until Lauren felt the tension gathering in her own body like a pent-up fever. Minutes or even hours passed as they were locked as one, sharing more than physical bodies, more than a sexual give and take.

Finn rocked with her, seeking a dark warmth within her with each long, deepening thrust. His passion escalated, his breathing became a pant that Lauren unconsciously echoed.

Then, too swiftly, much sooner than she wanted, Lauren clutched his shoulders. She couldn't stop it, couldn't withstand the heat, the tempo, the urgency yet one moment longer. The fever broke inside her with a violence, and she cried out at the limb-racking implosion of sensations. Her cry tore upward through her throat, and Finn was there to smother it at her lips, taking her mouth fiercely with his, while the powerful, pulsing surges of climax gradually diminished to tiny ripples that quivered in Lauren's veins. Finn steadied her, took her, then pressed deeper into her body once, twice more, twisting finally in a long, long moment of agonizing pleasure. He groaned her name and lay taut and still above her.

Slowly, they relaxed, melting once more into each other's arms, enveloping one another with returning awareness. He found her mouth in a soft kiss, and Lauren felt the fire in his lips subside into a gentle warmth.

Finn cradled her, holding her tenderly beneath his body, nuzzling her throat now and then but unable to put his thoughts into words. He was shy again. He couldn't find the way to say what he was feeling, she told herself. Rather than hear his thoughts through the voice of a cowboy or a Scottish prince or even Maurice, the foolish Frenchman, Lauren was also quiet. She smiled sleepily and wondered when she was going to hear from the real Finn Gallagher. How did the voice of the man who made love so eloquently sound?

In time, Finn slipped away from her, and they lay in warm, communing silence. He held her loosely, and his breathing turned rhythmic and long. Lauren kissed him whimsically on the nose, and his eyes opened.

"You're sleepy," she accused, smiling as she slid her legs comfortably between his.

"I'm sorry," he said, and his lashes slipped lower almost immediately. His smile was rueful, slow and bashful once again. He sighed, and it sounded contented. "I'm not usually this—this way."

"Don't disappoint me," Lauren coached, teasing him.

His smile was slower, sleepier still, and his arm wasn't

quite so strong as it had been. Finn was plummeting into sleep. He turned his head into her hair and murmured, "Stay with me?"

Lauren cuddled him, tucking her slender body snugly against his hard frame. "You couldn't chase me out, even if you had the strength. Have you been awake for days?"

"Two." He sighed again, but didn't move. In a moment, he added, slurred, "Maybe three. Lauren . . ."

"Hush. If you've been up for days, it's a wonder you even expressed an interest in anything but sleeping." Lauren smoothed his hair in her fingers, petting him gently. She laid her cheek against his and said thoughtfully, "You're an amazing man, Finn Gallagher. I don't understand you for the most part, and you're infuriating a lot of the time, but I—I really think I'm falling in love with you."

He didn't answer.

"Finn?"

He was asleep.

Lauren sighed and reached to tug the bedclothes up around the two of them. Finn slept with his nose buried in the pillow and one hand tucked under his ear, like a Norman Rockwell picture. Adorable. As she tucked him warmly into the blanket, Lauren whispered softly, "Yes, I'm sure I am. Good night, my love."

chapter 10

FINN SLEPT LIKE a man who'd been awake and working for a very long time. He didn't move, in fact, not even a wiggle all night. Lauren lay quietly with him, letting her mind wander peacefully until the street noises practically stopped and the building grew silent. She fell asleep curled against him and slept soundly.

The telephone woke her in the morning. Or rather it woke Finn, and when he sat up abruptly, startled, Lauren found herself blinking at his long, bare back.

"Yes," he said into the phone, sounding very wide awake.

He must get a lot of calls like this, Lauren thought. Nobody could sound so alert without a good deal of practice.

The caller spoke for a moment, and then Finn blew a slow, exasperated sigh. "Yes, George," he said patiently. "Now what? I ran the program through to you last night."

George, apparently, had a lot to say about the program.

Finn ran his hand through his tousled hair while he listened. After an instant, he broke in, saying seriously, "Are you speaking for the Pentagon now, George? What about Captain Kline's security clearance?"

Lauren sat up on one elbow, intrigued. The Pentagon calling Finn Gallagher on a Sunday morning? She listened to George's voice rise petulantly on the subject of Captain Kline.

"George," Finn said firmly to cut across the complaints, "George, wait. Don't panic. It will work, I promise. Jerry's working on that bug. It should be taken care of by this afternoon or I'll do it myself."

George shouted in frustration.

"Okay!" Finn exploded. "I'll have Steve pick up the disks and bring them here if it will make you happy. Yes, George. All right. Good-bye." Frowning, he hung up the phone.

Lauren lay back on the pillow, tugging the bedclothes to her chest. "Hi."

Finn sat for another moment on the edge of the bed. He was meditatively staring at the blank wall. "Hmm?"

"Good morning."

"Oh!" Finn exclaimed, and he spun around quickly, a smile starting. He lay down with her and wrapped his arms around her slim body. "Hi. Good morning. I'm sorry. Hello."

Lauren smiled and stroked his hair back from his forehead. His dark eyes were full of warm light and she found that she couldn't answer him right away. Just the expression on his face—so sweet, so open—gave her a wonderful rush of pleasure. That feeling must have been apparent in her expression, for Finn came closer and found her mouth with his. His kiss was soft and tentative, but it soon warmed. Lauren felt a surge of affection for him, and she lifted her arms around his neck and clasped his body to hers.

Their kiss was delightful, and they each unconsciously gathered the other closer, until Lauren's breasts were squished deliciously against Finn's chest, and his thigh slid slowly yet provocatively between her compliant knees. She smiled against Finn's mouth, then she gave a long and sated sigh.

Finn broke the kiss, also smiling. "Good morning. For real this time."

"Yes," Lauren agreed, touching his face with her forefinger and tracing a line down through the scruffy beard there. She wrinkled her nose at the sensation, but smiled. "Did you sleep well?"

"Wonderfully, thanks. I'm sorry I fell asleep like that. Very bad manners, I know. I'll do better."

"You spend a lot of hours at this tycoon business, don't you?"

"A few," Finn agreed shyly.

"A lot, I think."

"I guess so," he said. "More than I'd like sometimes. I haven't learned to say no." He touched a quick kiss to her mouth and drew away, looking uncomfortable suddenly. "Lauren . . ."

"No," she assured him before he could continue, "you didn't give away any company secrets in your sleep, I promise."

He smiled, but not with his eyes. "Listen, I know this is terrible, but would you hate me if I made one phone call?"

"Now?" she asked, surprised.

He nodded his head quickly. "I just—my head's going a mile a minute already with this thing—that phone call was important, and I—I'll feel better if I take care of—"

"All right," Lauren said with good humor. "I may be frustrated with you, but I won't hate you. Go ahead and call."

"Sure?" he asked anxiously, although he was already climbing around and reaching for the phone on the floor. "This will only take a second, I promise. If I don't do it now, I'll forget."

"I'll take that as a compliment," Lauren said wryly. "Or is it the Pentagon that has you occupied?"

He was punching buttons on the phone, but swiftly looked around at her. "What?"

"The Pentagon. That was a joke, wasn't it? You're not really working for the Pentagon, are you?"

Finn finished dialing and hooked the receiver between his shoulder and his ear. He glanced warily at Lauren, uncertain of her reaction. "Well, to be honest—yes."

"Finn! Really?"

"Sure," he said casually as the call went through. "I do

stuff for lots of people and organizations—government ones, too. The Pentagon hires me every now and then, but they act as if western civilization is going to collapse if I don't get things finished immediately, so unless it's really important, I don't—hello, Steve? Yeah, I'm sorry."

Steve swore, and Finn allowed him fifteen seconds' worth before breaking in. "Yes, Steve, I know. Listen, I need you," Finn said, turning away from Lauren. He winced as Steve continued to protest in no uncertain terms.

Smiling, Lauren began to trace a funny, tickling pattern down Finn's back, crisscrossing his spine and feathering the golden muscles on either side. He had such a nice body. He couldn't spend all his time sitting at a computer terminal, that was certain.

Finn wriggled to one side, trying to escape her fingertips. Half laughing, he said, "Okay, Steve, you got it. But not today. Run down to Kline's office and pick up some disks that George has for me. Yes, as soon as possible. No, not in Virginia. The downtown office. I know I could walk it, but I can't right now!" Finn grabbed Lauren's wrist and held her hard. He toppled backward on the bed, pinning her with his body. "Yes," he said breathlessly to Steve. "And pick me up some breakfast, okay? Lots. Look, I'm starving, that's all."

Finn put the receiver down on the telephone and buried it all in the jumble of bedclothes. He hesitated then, as if an idea had struck him. For a moment, he was lost in thought and staring at the wall again.

He was a million miles away, Lauren realized as she watched his pensively frowning profile. He was thinking about his program for the Pentagon already. Here she was in bed with a man who kept rabbits for pets and made beautiful love but would probably blush if she told him so, and his mind was already absorbed with his computer work. She was naked and there was nothing but a tangled sheet between them, and he was thinking about disks and circuits and who knew what else!

She touched Finn's shoulder to get his attention. He had

his back to her still, but he turned his head a little—he was not quite out of his trance yet. Lauren said, "You're working, and it's not even eight o'clock yet."

He gave her an automatic smile and thoughtfully placed his hand on the long undercurve of her thigh. "I'm sorry."

"This happens a lot, doesn't it?"

"The phone? I guess most of the work I do for people manages to get complicated at weird hours. Either two in the morning or—" He looked at her fully and began again with sincerity, "Listen, I'm sorry, Lauren, about the phone calls. Everybody knows this is a good time to catch me here. I don't usually have visitors at this time of day."

"I'm glad."

Finn tipped his head and smiled genuinely at her. "I am, too."

Lauren pulled him by the shoulders until he was once more comfortably nestled against her body in the bed. She slipped her fingers tentatively along the line of his arms and strangely found that she could not meet his eyes. "Finn . . . about last night . . ."

"That tone of voice sounds ominous," he said immediately.

She smiled. "It isn't ominous. I just—well, I feel funny that we didn't talk about—about all kinds of things before we ended up here."

"Hmm," murmured Finn, dipping his head until he could press a small kiss to her shoulder. "That's my fault."

"It doesn't have to be anyone's fault," Lauren protested. "But we can both work at correcting it."

"Yes, Doctor."

Startled by his sudden sarcasm, Lauren didn't move for a split second.

"I'm sorry," Finn said quickly, his grip tightening on her. "I didn't mean to sound flip. This kind of talk is your territory, that's all. Not mine. I'm not good at this stuff, Laurie."

"You're better than you think," Lauren said softly, watching his eyes. She saw dismay, concern, and sheer nervousness come and go in his face in the time it takes most people to blink. To encourage him, she repeated, "Much better, Finn."

"Not to hear my wife talk," Finn said with false cheer. "She used to complain about my complete lack of social graces, and I haven't improved much since—" Finn caught himself.

With her palms on his chest, Lauren pushed him back from her until she could see his expression. Without thinking, she demanded, "Your *what?*"

His eyes were wide with amazement at what he had just said. He gulped and asked, "I guess I should have mentioned her before?"

"Your *wife?*" Lauren repeated. "You were married?"

"A long time ago," Finn explained swiftly. "I was only twenty years old. Should I have said something earlier? I haven't seen her for a long time. Eight years, at least. Oh, boy. I've knocked you for a loop, haven't I? Is that important now?"

"No," Lauren said slowly, her mind clearing. She could feel her smile begin to return, but it was suddenly stiff around the edges. "It was just a shock to hear you say you had a wife once, that's all."

"Oh, boy," Finn groaned. "Lauren, I—"

"It doesn't make a difference, Finn," she assured him before he could start berating himself. She tried to smile and said, "In fact, it kind of explains a few things."

He was watching her face cautiously, as if half expecting her to make a final and unfavorable judgment about him. "What things?"

Lauren could not bring herself to tell him. A man doesn't become a tiger in bed by reading books any more than he becomes a computer tycoon by sitting passively at his flickering green screen. Finn wasn't too good at interacting with people, but the lessons he had learned, he'd learned perfectly. Lauren petted him gently. "Never mind. You surprised me. Again. You've been married, huh?"

He nodded, cupping her shoulders in his hands very gently. "So long ago that I hardly remember what it was like. I—it was in California."

Tender territory, Lauren guessed. Not sure she should be asking at all, but unable to stop herself for doing just a little exploring, Lauren asked neutrally, "What's her name?"

Finn smiled shyly. "Kimberly."

Lauren giggled. "Kimberly? Really? Did she surf, too?"

He laughed uneasily. "Yep. What's the matter? Don't you think I'd hit it off with a golden girl called Kimberly?"

Amused, Lauren shook her head. "A graduate from Smith with a name like Jane would be more your style, I think. How'd it happen?"

"My marriage? It was kind of like Mauna Loa, as a matter of fact."

Giggling, Lauren hugged him. "Lots of steam, huh?"

"I was thinking of explosive," Finn corrected, trying to be serious. But he had to smile, and added, "Come to think of it, though, things were pretty steamy for a while, too!"

Lauren met his sparkling eyes and suggested, "Long nights on the beach, huh?"

Finn shuddered, remembering. "There was sand in everything we owned, as a matter of fact. Ouch! What a disaster. The whole thing."

"I'll bet your mother told you so."

"My mother," said Finn wisely, "kept her nose out of it. I learned that lesson all by myself."

"What happened?" Lauren asked when curiosity got the best of her. "To you and Kimberly, I mean?"

"I was careless," Finn confessed without delay.

Lauren tipped her head inquiringly.

Finn fondled her shoulders and said, "I guess I needed to see someone like you then—a professional, I mean. It was my fault. I didn't pay attention to things when I should have, and she finally got disgusted and left. I sure didn't blame her."

"Oh, Finn."

"Honest, I'm long over that relationship," he added quickly. "I goofed and let her go. She said I wasn't able to organize my life into priorities, and she was right."

"And now?"

"Now?" Finn repeated, visibly surprised by the question. He was quiet for a long time then—considering his response carefully, Lauren surmised. Out of instinct, she wound her arms around his neck for support. She held him, and after a time, Finn looked her straight in her eyes and said, "I don't know."

The phone rang.

"I don't believe it," said Lauren in exasperation.

"I'm sorry!" cried Finn.

"You've said you're sorry forty times already this morning."

"I'm—" Finn grabbed up the phone to silence it and couldn't stop the next word in time, "—sorry."

Lauren laughed and shoved him off her.

Finn put the receiver to his ear and said, "Hang on a minute."

Lauren sat up beside him. "I think I'm about to be asked to leave."

"No, Laurie."

"I'm not being thrown out?"

He tipped her head up to his and kissed her gently. "No, of course not."

"Should I go anyway?" she asked, looking into his eyes directly and hoping her blunt question would elicit an honest answer. "I can tell you're going to work all day, right?"

"Well, Pilgrim," Finn said, tucking the phone into his hand and assuming the identity of John Wayne with a sudden drawl and a phony sideways grin down at her, "you're welcome to stay here on the old homestead. Females are mighty scarce around these parts."

"But . . . ?"

"No buts about it, ma'am. Womenfolk ain't exactly a distraction I object to."

Lauren was silent. Sometimes the accents and the character routines were a bit annoying. And bed was the last place Lauren wanted to share with yet another of Finn's peculiar characters. "Finn," she pressed with more patience than she was really feeling, "if you need to work this morning, then just tell me to go home, and I'll see you again when you've got the time and the inclination."

"Darlin', I've got plenty of inclination," Finn teased her, coming close to give her a quick, searing kiss on the mouth. "But it's startin' to look like my time's kinda short today, and I'd hate to be accused of mistreatin' a little filly like yourself."

The "little filly" was about to kick him by that time, but Lauren managed to restrain herself. This morning had been one of the few times when Finn had given up his silly pretenses for a while and truly communicated with her, man to woman. For once their conversation had been intimate. It had been an uphill struggle to draw shy Finnegan Gallagher out and get him to confide in her—to speak from his heart. Lauren could see that the mood had been spoiled. She wasn't capable of coaxing him back to that kind of reflective conversation all over again. She gave up and gestured at the receiver with barely disguised annoyance. "Answer your call."

Finn obeyed without a second thought. "Yes? Oh, Jerry. Sorry for the delay. Yeah, George already called. He pushed the panic button and everything's breaking loose. Yes, I'll help. Plug in and we'll try some tricks. I've got all day."

That did it. There were times to answer the phone and times to let it go. There were times to politely ask the caller to call back later, and the middle of a discussion about his ex-wife was definitely one of those. Lauren pushed and got out from under Finn while he continued his conversation with Jerry. Lauren climbed out of bed and gathered up her clothes, then headed for the bathroom.

"Wait a minute," Finn said into the phone.

Lauren hesitated in the doorway, hopeful.

But Finn was still talking to Jerry. "Let me run her through my system and we'll check," he said. "If she crashes, we haven't lost too much, right?"

Lauren's hopes plummeted, but she continued to watch Finn for a moment. He folded up his long legs and sat cross-legged in the bed, rubbing his forehead and thinking hard.

He was working, and she had been forgotten.

Lauren went into the bathroom and closed the door. She began to wonder if she had made a very large mistake.

When she had finished dressing, Lauren went in search of Finn once more and found him already at his computer terminal. He had pulled on his faded jeans again and had snapped open the top on a can of orange soda. He sipped from it, with yet another telephone receiver clamped between his ear and shoulder. He was still talking with Jerry, it seemed, and quickly tapped out a message on his keyboard.

"Okay," he said, sitting back to watch the screen with a critical eye. "Roll her, my friend."

There are some men, Lauren thought, who are so wonderful that you begin to wonder what could possibly be wrong with them. The perfect man has to have a flaw somewhere. As she watched Finn set to work on his computer problem, she realized that she had just discovered Finn's major flaw. If he had been a nail-biter or a collector of a rare breed of tropical spotted rabbits, she could have coped somehow. But this was a different story. A man who was obsessed—perhaps in love was a better way of putting it— with his work, wasn't going to have an easy time sharing himself with a woman. A lady had to be understanding, but this might be too much for even a professional understander to take.

Watching his screen, Finn said into the phone, "Go easy, Jer. Let's be careful with her, all right?"

He even called his programs "her."

Lauren went out through the hallway, gathered up her handbag, and, almost as an afterthought, switched on Finn's tape machine once more. As the Rolling Stones got revved up with "I can't get no satisfaction," Lauren let herself out the door and started down the steps. Well, Mick, she thought, sometimes you're a real philosopher.

Steve met her on the landing. He was half-asleep, wearing a scroungy Windbreaker and balancing two Styrofoam trays in one upturned hand. He didn't look surprised when he recognized Lauren above him.

"Good morning," she said coolly, continuing down the stairs.

"Well, look who's here," Steve remarked with a cocky grin.

"Nice to see you again," Lauren answered, though her tone of voice hardly matched her gracious words.

"Hey, don't run off," Steve said. "This is your breakfast, after all. If I'd known it was you he was with this time, I'd have brought a snooty newspaper for you to read in the sack."

Ignore him, Lauren commanded herself. Just keep going and don't listen.

Steve blocked her path, holding out the breakfast tray. "Here, take it. It's paid for."

Lauren pushed the tray back. "Give it to Finn. He can use the extra energy."

"Oh-ho," Steve said on a laugh. "You tired him out, you mean? You must be more woman than the others he's had up and down these steps in the last few years."

Lauren couldn't stop herself from an automatic response to Steve's repulsive suggestion. "What others?"

Steve smiled and shrugged. "Lots. Man, that guy gets more chicks than anybody I know. It's the big bucks that gets 'em interested, and he does the rest somehow. Which routine did he pull on you? The Texas ranger? Or the sweet and innocent act?"

Lauren didn't speak as she moved to push past the loathsome Steve.

"My money's on the shy, naive routine every time," he went on. "He's got that act down to a science. I never figured a smart lady doctor like you would fall for it, though."

Lauren was trembling. She knew it was stupid to listen, stupid to ask, but she couldn't stop. "Are you suggesting that Finn Gallagher is—is—"

"A lady-killer? A hound? The biggest make-out artist since—hey, Doc, let me tell you. I see everything, remem-

ber? I drive, sail, cook, clean—all that stuff—so he's got
enough time to keep the ladies happy. The guy's amazing!
I wish I had half his technique."

Enough. Lauren cut around the newel post and hurried
down the stairs.

A door slammed below her, and Steve bent over the
railing to see who it was. "Hey, Betsy!" he called.

A red-haired woman who looked about twenty-seven was
climbing the stairs. She turned onto the landing just as
Lauren started down. She was wearing a bathrobe—not a
slinky one, but a bathrobe nevertheless. She wasn't very
tall, but Lauren realized belatedly that she was wearing
bedroom slippers. She had taken time to comb her hair and
put on a little makeup. There was a thick, unread newspaper
in her hands, and she held it protectively before her slim
body as she eyed Lauren with a mixture of surprise and
suspicion.

"Well, isn't this a touchy situation?" Steve asked slyly.

"Hello," Betsy said to Lauren.

Lauren was blushing in spite of the fierce inner lecture
she was giving herself. Don't look guilty, don't act nervous.
It's just a chance encounter of two women on a staircase,
she told herself. But she was very aware that the man they
both just happened to be interested in was in the apartment
above them. Lauren gathered her composure and managed
to say a civil, "Good morning," before continuing down the
staircase.

"Boy," said Steve, "that was disappointing. Can't we
have a little cat fight? I love that stuff."

"Steve," Lauren heard Betsy say sweetly, "go take that
limousine and drive to France, will you? The direct route.
You're such a moron!"

In the next second Lauren was out on the street and almost
running for her car. What a morning! Yet, it had all been
so wonderful last night. She unlocked the door and threw
it open. Safe inside her car, she slammed the door again
and slumped against the wheel, breathing hard.

Could Steve be telling the truth? Surely not! Finn? A
make-out king? It couldn't possibly be true. After all, he'd

nearly run screaming from her that night they kissed in the hotel door! Wouldn't a more experienced man have marched her right back inside the hotel and taken her to the nearest room?

Maybe not, Lauren reasoned coldly. Your Honor, the prosecution suggests that Mr. Finnegan Gallagher knew full well that Dr. Chambers wasn't going to fall into bed with him so easily. He had played that scene carefully—knowing that he had a better chance of seducing the innocent Lauren Chambers if he waited and allowed her temperature to rise of its own accord. Since he is so accomplished at seducing women, he—

No, no. It was foolish to start imagining things. After all, hadn't Finn been kind and sweet right up until they were making love in his bed?

Then Lauren's more cynical side remembered the skill, the talent Finn had displayed in bed. He had been wonderful, in fact. A man didn't become a terrific lover without a little practice.

But wait, pleaded Lauren's gentler half. He'd been married. He certainly could have learned how to please a woman while he was married to the surfer girl. Right?

Lauren's arguing alter egos came to a screeching halt. Finn's wife. He hadn't called her his *ex*-wife. He had called her his wife. Good Lord, could he still be married?

With that thought branded in her brain, Lauren started her car and headed for home. This definitely called for some double-chocolate ice cream and an afternoon of solitude. There was too much to think about.

When she got home, Philip called.

chapter 11

"OH, PHILIP," LAUREN said into the phone. "I'm terribly sorry, but I just can't talk to you at the moment. I—I'm not feeling very well."

"I'm so sorry," Philip said. "Is there anything I can do?"

She told him there wasn't, and after hanging up wondered if Finn would have asked that question. Or was he too self-centered to think of others? So far, he had alternately displayed a single-minded determination to establish Lauren as a part of his life and a complete disregard for her existence! Had Finn become one of those egocentric men who liked sex with many women but intimacy with none of them? Lauren didn't like the role she was being given in this relationship. She was expected to drop Philip without a moment's notice and run off with Finn whenever he chose, but *he* was making no similar sacrifices! It wasn't fair. Not to Lauren, and certainly not to Philip, a man who deserved better treatment than he was getting.

Finn was being irresponsible, and after her love affair with Josh Redmond, Lauren didn't like the idea of chasing after a man to get the love and commitment she needed. She had lost her dignity when Josh went off to New York, and she'd be darned if she was going to pursue Finn the way she had Josh. She could only humiliate herself all over again. No, she needed some answers from Finn before things went any further.

But, curses—he didn't telephone again!

Lauren spent a week thinking about Finn, mulling over the possibilities. And he didn't call to change her opinion, either. That did it! He hadn't phoned her last week, but had jumped at the chance to sleep with her when the opportunity arose. Now he wasn't calling again!

Lauren felt angry, and then betrayed. In her view, making love required a certain amount of trust, and Finn violated that trust every day that went by without his telephoning. So when Philip phoned again on Thursday afternoon, she was much more receptive.

"Hello!" she said, mustering some good cheer.

"Did I catch you between clients?" Philip asked.

"Just. This seems to be a busy week for me. I'm swamped. How are you, Philip?"

"I'm ready for a vacation, as a matter of fact. How about you?"

Lauren laughed. "Count me in. I could use a week on a beach, that's for sure."

"Well," Philip said gallantly, "I can't offer you a whole week, but how does a weekend sound?"

Lauren sat up in her swivel chair, totally alert. "What?"

"I'm serious," Philip said. "I know that you and I haven't had much of a chance to get to know each other, mostly because of that strange Gallagher friend of yours, so I've got a suggestion. I hope you won't think I've got something up my sleeve, Lauren, but I was just talking to my travel agent. He made a reservation for me at a hotel on an island off South Carolina, and on a whim, I told him to sign me up for two rooms. What do you say?"

Lauren sat still in her chair. "Uh, Philip . . ."

"I know it sounds very forward of me, but I thought this was probably the only way to get you to myself for more

than half an hour. Two rooms, I promise. The plane leaves
Friday afternoon at five-thirty, and we're booked. What do
you say? The temperature's eighty-five and the beach is
beautiful."

"Keep talking," Lauren coached with a grin.

"Fine restaurants, a little tennis, maybe some dancing
Saturday evening—"

"You've convinced me," Lauren capitulated. "Philip,
this is so impulsive!"

"I'm learning," Philip said grimly. "If I've got to keep
up with young fellows like Gallagher, I had better try using
some imagination. Really? Will you come with me?"

"Yes," Lauren said firmly, plucking the paper daisy from
her desk. Glaring at it, she said, "I'd love to get away,
Philip. What time did you say the plane leaves?"

"Five-thirty. United flight three-one-three. It's an economy flight, but if you're feeling the way I am at the moment,
I'd swim to the island! I'll meet you at the airport. Pack
your bathing suit."

Lauren threw the flower down on her desk. "I'll be there!"

If Finn tried to call over the weekend, she was going to
be out. To hell with him! Lauren spent Thursday night
packing and repacking a suitcase and alternately hoping and
dreading that the phone was going to ring and she'd hear
Finn's voice. He did not call, however, and Lauren was
past getting in touch with him.

So, after work on Friday, she took a cab to the airport
and found herself sitting in the waiting area and looking for
Philip. She sat in a row of uncomfortable plastic seats and
involuntarily began to feel guilty.

After all, here she had impulsively agreed to go away
for the weekend with a man she'd hardly spent more than
a few hours with. Granted, he had made his pure intentions
very clear, but this was still a big step for Lauren. She didn't
usually drop everything and go chasing off for romantic
weekends.

She didn't sleep with computer whiz kids at the drop of
a hat, either. Boy, was her head in a muddle! With images
of Finn competing with her own worries about her recent

behavior, things were getting out of hand. Blast Finnegan T. Gallagher, anyway!

Sitting alone, Lauren started thinking of him again. Hardly an hour went by anymore when she didn't. What was wrong with him? If he were her client, how would the objective Dr. Chambers evaluate a man like Finn? With an inward wry grin, Lauren began to dictate notes in her head. Friday evening. Baltimore airport. Client: Finn Gallagher. Diagnosis: Unclear, pending further research. Notes: Mr. Gallagher has displayed all the signs of a healthy young man with normal career goals and a fluctuating but active sex life. He abuses himself, but not in ways that most people recognize. No drugs, but certainly denies himself regular sleep, exercise, and nutritious food. Probably a workaholic who spares little time for relaxation. Question: Is Mr. Gallagher too infatuated with his work to truly love someone? Is he incapable of maintaining a monogamous relationship with a woman? The breakup of his brief marriage—whether he is formally divorced or not—is proof that he was once incapable of devoting the time and energy to another person. Is that still the case? Is he happy with his work and occasional forays into short sexual liaisons? Is he not the perfect candidate for that blasted dating service he owns? Eating junk food and enjoying similar relationships with women?

Her flight number was called, and Lauren gathered up her carry-on bag. She headed for the jetway, still engrossed in thought. No, if Finn cared for her at all, he would have called. He couldn't have let a week go by this way—not after making love on Saturday night! Not even he could be so inadequate!

"Miss?" inquired the uniformed young man at the entrance to the jetway.

Lauren snapped out of her mental fog and showed her ticket. "What? Oh, yes. Flight three-one-three to South Carolina, right?"

"Right," he told her with a smile. "But the first-class passengers can wait until the other seats are filled. It will just take a minute, and you can wait here where it's less crowded."

"First class?" Lauren looked at her ticket. "Are you sure? Someone else made the reservations, and I'm sure he said that we'd be taking an economy flight."

Patiently, the man flipped the ticket folder over and showed her. "See? First class. I'm sure you'd like it better than economy, but if you want me to check, I'll go look at the computer."

"Computer?" Lauren repeated stupidly, staring at him.

The young man obviously had plenty of experience with unnerved passengers, so he patted her arm and said, "Just wait over there, miss. We'll call you in a minute."

A computer. First class instead of economy. Oh, no. Could Finn—? Would he—? How could he have—?

No, no, Dr. Chambers, it's just your overactive imagination. Philip is going to turn up any minute, and you're going to take off for a quiet weekend on a sunny island. You can think about Finn Gallagher when you get back on Monday.

But Philip didn't come. Minutes ticked by, and the line of passengers heading into the jetway grew shorter and shorter. Lauren tapped her foot and began searching the crowded lounge with her eyes. What was keeping Philip?

The uniformed young man motioned to Lauren. "We're ready for you, miss."

"But my friend," Lauren objected. "He isn't here yet!"

"The plane won't take off for another ten minutes," the attendant told her. "Perhaps he's just caught in traffic."

Well, the ticket was paid for, Lauren thought. She could reimburse Philip for it if he didn't make the flight, she supposed. Spending a weekend waiting for the phone to ring sounded too depressing. And she'd been hoping for exactly this kind of getaway weekend for months now! Determined to go and get Finn out of her mind no matter what, Lauren picked up her bag and stepped into the jetway. She started for the plane.

There was only one other person in the first-class section of the airplane, a small, middle-aged woman who glanced up from her *Wall Street Journal* and gave Lauren's shocking-pink resort dress a disapproving look before going back to her reading. Lauren put her handbag on the seat farthest from the woman and set about stowing her suitcase in the overhead compartment. The flight attendants were all busy settling the economy-class passengers, stocking the drinks tray, and closing the hatch.

"Hold it! Wait!"

"Your ticket, sir?"

"It's here somewhere. I just had it—check my back pocket, will you? It's got to be—oh, thanks."

Oh, no. Here we go again. Grimly, Lauren turned.

"Hi," said Finn, snatching off his cowboy hat. He swooped and gave her a hard, noisy kiss on the mouth. "I made it."

"Where is Philip?" Lauren demanded, clapping the back of her hand automatically to her burning mouth and glaring like a cornered wildcat.

"Downtown," Finn said, panting. He was dressed in jeans, running shoes, a T-shirt that read SAINT MARY'S, over which he had thrown a navy sports jacket. He had a carry-on bag slung over one shoulder and he looked as if he had just flown in on a tornado—hair windblown and his dark eyes sparkling with adrenaline. "He's got to work late."

"Philip is working?" Lauren was suspicious and angry immediately. "Finn, what have you done?"

"Nothing," he said right away, easing her backward with a hand on each of her hips. "Nothing much. It was painless, honestly, Laurie. He's going to thank me some day. Sit down."

"Finn," Lauren objected murderously, jerking out from under his grasp, "if you lay a hand on me, I'm going to clobber you with the first thing I can lay *my* hands on!"

"This?" He pulled a bright-orange paper rose from his sleeve.

"Don't you dare try to dazzle me with that magic stuff again!" She dashed his hand away. "I've had it with you!"

"Laurie—"

"I mean it, Finn. You've ignored me and you're doing something mean to Philip again, I know you are!"

"Don't be angry," Finn pleaded, pocketing the rose and trying to catch his breath just as quickly. "Listen to me first, okay? Wait until we're off the ground, and I'll—"

"If you think I have the slightest inclination to spend the weekend with you, you had better—better—just—"

The lady with *The Wall Street Journal* was looking more than disapproving by now. And the passengers in the first few economy seats were sitting eagerly forward, listening. The nearest stewardess was smiling, and Lauren abruptly flushed with embarrassment.

"See?" Finn said softly, taking her elbow. "You're only making a scene. I'll explain, I promise. Sit down. Fasten your seat belt."

"I'm not going anywhere with you." Lauren repeated, though she had backed automatically into the seat. She picked up Finn's hat and sat down with the Stetson in her lap.

"I understand," Finn said, full of sympathy. He shoved his own bag into the overhead compartment before sliding into the seat beside her. He flipped up the armrest that separated their seats. "In fact, I wouldn't be surprised if you hauled off and hit me with a rolled-up magazine. But you're too much of a lady for that. I don't deserve such nice treatment. Laurie, I'm sorry—"

"Lauren!" she corrected adamantly, gripping the brim of his hat with her fingernails. "My name is Lauren!"

"Yes—"

"And I may not be a lady much longer if you keep it up, buster."

"Oh, boy," moaned Finn. "This is worse than I thought. Laurie—"

"Lauren!" she shouted.

"Lauren," he agreed hastily. "I had to see you. This week has been terrible for me, and when I realized Wednesday had come and gone before I had a minute to call you—"

"But you didn't even call me on Wednesday!" Lauren cried. "How could you be such an unfeeling rat?"

"I was a rat," he said, taking her hand in his and fighting

to hold it, "but I wasn't unfeeling. On Wednesday I knew I had to do something drastic, but on Thursday I had another emergency, so I had to work fast. Philip's fine."

"Where is he?" Lauren asked, jerking to free her hand from his.

"At his bank," Finn explained quickly. "Something went wrong with the vault and—"

"Did you cause it? You and your cursed computer? Did you, Finn?"

"Yes," he said, and he braced for her furious reaction.

"Oh, Finn!" Lauren cried. "That was horrible! Rotten! You can't control people this way! You—you—poor Philip had a wonderful weekend planned, and you've ruined it! He really needed to get away, and you've spoiled his plans! I really—*really* dislike you for that, Finn!"

He squished his eyes closed. "Oh, this is much, much worse than I thought. I feel terrible. I made it as nice as I could, honestly. He's got company in there, and there's food and a bottle of—"

"What!"

Finn blinked at her anxiously. "He'll be okay, I promise."

"Finn, wait a minute," Lauren said loudly. "Do you mean that you've actually locked Philip in the *vault?*"

Finn swallowed hard and looked sick.

"You didn't!"

He nodded.

Lauren was aghast. "Finn, how *could* you?"

"It wasn't hard. It's going to open tonight, in fact. I could have left him locked in there all weekend, but I just rigged it for a few hours. And Sally's there, so he won't be—"

"Sally!"

"Remember her? She helped me with the magic at the concert that night. She had to check a safety-deposit box anyway, and when I knew that I simply asked her to go see Philip and ask if he'd take care of her personally. It was easy to rig the timers so that when Philip checked his security code into the vault system, it triggered the whole thing to—"

"I don't believe it," Lauren moaned, burying her face in her hands.

"And I gave Sally a weekend trip to Nassau, with an extra ticket for Philip. Unfortunately, it has to be next weekend, because Sally has something to do in Baltimore tomorrow, but they'll have a great time and it won't cost him a cent."

"You can't buy people!" Lauren shouted.

"I know," Finn said contritely. "But they like each other. He asked her to go with him this weekend before he asked you, but she couldn't because she'd already made plans for tomorrow. She was his first choice, after all, Laur—" He caught himself and chose to get her name right for safety's sake. "Lauren."

Lauren eyed him, frowning. "And what do you think of that?"

"What? Sally and Philip?"

"No, me going to this island with Philip after Sally refused."

"Oh," Finn said comfortably. "You agreed to go with him because you're mad at me, not because you like Philip all that much."

Lauren clenched her teeth to prevent her scream of frustration. She held back so bone-shakingly hard that her whole body was trembling with rage. Furiously, she squashed Finn's hat in her hands and threw it into the aisle.

Finn looked down at his mangled hat. "Wow. You're upset."

"Darn right. I'd do that to your head if there weren't so many witnesses."

Finn smiled. "Boy, I love you."

"Don't say that!" Lauren cried, clapping her hands over her ears.

"I can't help it. I do, Lauren, and I want to kiss you even though you're so angry."

"I'll bite you!"

"Then I'm masochistic. Hey, you look wonderful. Pink." He cast a long, appreciative look at her pretty outfit. "You look gorgeous, in fact."

"Stop it."

"All right. I'll stop. Fasten your seat belt before I do it for you. I want to touch you."

"Stop it!" Lauren commanded, grabbing up the ends of her seat belt before he could. "I'm not going to make a scene here, but I don't want to go anywhere with you right now."

"You're just angry," Finn said, buckling up.

"You're darn right I am. And I've got good reason. I fully intend to take the first flight back here to Baltimore if you won't leave me alone."

"Let's talk first, okay?" Abruptly, Finn became the Texas ranger again. "Please, ma'am? After y'all wounded my pore lil' hat, I jes'—"

"Cut it with that accent right now or I *will* make a scene!"

"Lauren—"

"I mean it, Finn, I'm fed up with your crazy characters and all the men you pretend to be!"

Surprised, Finn said, "Lauren, I don't pretend to be anybody but me."

"Then why can't you just be yourself instead of hiding behind all those ridiculous accents?" she demanded.

"It's just a habit—"

"If you want to talk, then talk like Finn Gallagher, not like some dopey cowpoke. Got that?"

Finn folded his hands in his lap and looked down. His voice lost its verve suddenly. "Okay."

"And don't go all immature on me!" Lauren exclaimed in exasperation. "Honestly, Finn, you can't possibly have such a thin skin as you pretend!"

Finn was silent.

"Curses!" Lauren cried, clenching her teeth in frustration and pounding her fists in her lap. "Talk to me, dammit, or I'm going to get off this plane this instant!"

"What do you want to know?" Finn asked quickly. "How

come you're so upset, Laurie?"

"How come—?" Lauren stared at him. "Haven't you the faintest idea?"

"If it's about Sunday morning and for not calling you again this week, I can only say—"

"I'm sorry," Lauren finished rudely. "Yes, I know."

"Look," Finn said suddenly, "I think you need to cool down."

Lauren sat up straight in outrage. "How dare you, of all people, tell me to—"

"I mean it," Finn said sharply, staring her down. "You're upset, and I'm to blame, but you're saying things you don't mean, and that's as bad as what I did. Take it easy for a few minutes, okay? Just relax."

Lauren glared at him a moment longer, her brain going completely blank.

The stewardess arrived just in time then to save the argument from going any further. Finn turned away from Lauren and said hello to the young woman. She rescued Finn's mauled cowboy hat and asked about drinks and magazines. Making chitchat, she set about seeing to their comforts before the takeoff. Lauren watched in stony silence. The stewardess was charmed by Finn and tried to draw him into conversation. He was friendly with her, but still just a little shy.

Listening to his slow responses to the attractive young woman, Lauren started wondering anew. Just what kind of a man was he, for crying out loud? She put her face to the window. Oh, brother, old girl. Now what?

The flight was a short one, thankfully. And during that time, Finn was very quiet. He talked to the stewardess who was assigned to the first-class section of the plane, and he reached to hold Lauren's hand when the plane took off and landed. Other than that, he did not try to speak to her.

Naturally, Lauren's heart began to melt. She had hurt his feelings. She had been angry because he hadn't called her. Maybe he had a good excuse. He didn't know about the things Steve had told her. And he didn't know of Lauren's concern about Betsy, the woman who visited him in her bathrobe, and Kimberly, his wife or ex-wife, whichever she was.

Finn was quiet and Lauren began to feel guilty. They did not speak. Like a couple of teenage steadies who were having a spat, they didn't talk during the whole flight.

The plane landed and Finn got Lauren's suitcase down for her. He shouldered his own bag, said good-bye to the stewardess, and shook hands with the pilot who stood by the hatchway. He followed Lauren out of the plane, and in the airport took her elbow.

"There's a limousine for the hotel," he said calmly to her when they reached the airport concourse together. "This way."

Still silent, Lauren let him take command of the situation. They found the van that shuttled patrons from the airport to the island, and with half a dozen other chattering passengers, they rode through the dusky night for about thirty minutes. When the hotel lights appeared, Lauren was relieved. She was tired and feeling very vulnerable where Finn was concerned.

And, for some reason, she wanted to cry.

Finn checked them in. The desk clerk sent a surreptitious look up and down Finn's casual outfit, but said nothing and politely called a porter to carry their bags. Lauren surrendered hers and let Finn hold her by the hand while they followed the man out into the night again.

The hotel was a large white beachfront building that was illuminated by spectacular spotlights that bounced off the palm trees and played games in the shadows. The breeze was cool and slightly fishy smelling, and Lauren unconsciously turned her face to the sea as they walked. With her hand captured warmly in Finn's and the ocean breeze so silky on her face, she was suddenly glad she had come.

They walked along a gravel-paved sidewalk under a vibrant yellow awning canopy, around a pool where a young couple had come for a sunset swim. The sky was growing darker every moment. The tall, slanting lines of a series of condominiums appeared through the palms, and the porter led them in that direction. The condos were just fifty yards from the washing surf and were much quieter than the hotel. In fact, Lauren guessed that they were the only guests staying there so early in the season.

"I'm starving," Finn said when the porter left them alone outside their respective doors. "Will you at least have dinner with me? You don't have to talk if you don't want to."

Lauren tapped her foot. "I'll talk to you after I've had a chance to figure out how I feel. In the meantime, yes, I'll have dinner with you. But I'd like to take a shower and have some time alone first."

"Okay," Finn agreed, opening her door for her. "In an hour? I'll call for a reservation somewhere."

"That will be fine," Lauren said grandly, and she passed into the sitting room of her condo. Without another word to Finn, she closed the door. She heard his door close a moment later.

What to do? From the moment he'd met her, Finn had been playing these silly stunts to get her attention. He'd humiliated Philip, used this Sally woman, and manipulated Lauren herself in half a dozen ways to get what he wanted. Until now she had thought that his pranks were essentially harmless. But locking Philip in a bank vault wasn't nice. In fact, it could be downright dangerous. What if Philip had a heart attack? Or Sally, for that matter? Or the bank caught fire? Finn just hadn't considered the potential consequences. He'd acted like a spoiled little boy, and it wasn't funny.

On the other hand, he'd done it out of genuine feeling for her, Lauren mused. He'd orchestrated this weekend with her because he loved her. He said he loved her, anyway, and that was very flattering.

It was more than flattering. It gave her hope. Maybe, just maybe, if he was carefully pointed in the right direction, Finn might shape up into quite a guy.

Was it possible to change a man, though? And if she could change Finn, would he still retain that unique boyish charm that set him so far apart from other men?

Lauren threw her handbag at the pillows on the bed. "Oh, curses, Mr. Finnegan T. Gallagher! Why couldn't you have just allowed me to go through with your blasted dating-service experience and let it go at that?"

The pillow made no response, though, so Lauren marched into the bathroom and turned on the shower full blast. She undressed and got under the hot water, still thinking. The first rule, Dr. Chambers, is to communicate. You can't solve this problem alone. Talk to the man.

Lauren got dressed again, slowly. She reapplied her makeup and brushed her hair. She unpacked. At the appointed hour, she went out the door, key in hand, to look for Finn.

He was on the beach. She could see his tall, lanky silhouette down at the water's edge, kicking at shells and looking out at the quiet ocean. She pulled off her shoes and carried them as she walked through the gritty white sand.

He didn't speak when she arrived on the harder-packed sand, but he lifted his head and watched her. His dark eyes were in shadow, but Lauren knew they were serious, perhaps even full of misgivings. He had put on a button-down shirt and tie this time, and he'd combed his hair—though the breeze had already begun to recreate his usual hairstyle. He looked charmingly young and sweetly uneasy, like a teenager about to greet his prom date.

"Hello," Lauren said, trying to sound calm. Her heart was suddenly acting crazy, though. And she couldn't quite breathe right. The sea air must be too exhilarating, she supposed.

"Hi," Finn breathed.

"Still hungry?"

He nodded, but didn't speak.

"Shall we go?"

But Finn hesitated. He looked down at his feet, then out at the ocean. "Lauren . . ."

She waited.

Finn sighed. "Look, I know I keep saying this, but I'm sorry. You must be tired of hearing it. I just—" He kicked hard at a shell and sent it skittering into the whispery wash of surf. He looked at her, then said abruptly, "If you're sick of me and the things I've done, I wouldn't blame you. If you want me to go, I'll leave tonight and you can have the rest of the weekend to recuperate."

Lauren hugged her arms around her body, suddenly chilled by the breeze. She sighed. "Oh, Finn."

"I'm a pain in the neck," he continued. "And I haven't grown up yet. I may never grow up, in fact, so maybe this—this whole thing is a lost cause. I don't think I'm ever going to be the kind of man that you—well, that you could—"

"Don't," Lauren interrupted quietly. "Don't belittle yourself, Finn. I like you just the way you are, honestly. But you get carried away sometimes, and that isn't good. What you did to Philip tonight was downright awful."

"I called," Finn said miserably. "He's okay."

"Really?" Lauren asked, voice rising. "Is he all right?"

"He's mad, of course. But he's okay."

"Did you talk directly to him?"

"Yes," said Finn. "But if you don't mind, I don't think I'll repeat that conversation just yet, okay?"

Lauren studied him for a moment. He had obviously spent the last hour thinking as hard as she had. He had come to some conclusions about himself, too. He was full of remorse, she could see. And clearly Philip had chewed him out royally. This was a Finn who was feeling inadequate and sorry and worried.

Lauren reached out and took his arm. She stepped close to him to seek his body heat. Tipping her head up to him, she said, "Let's go get some dinner, okay? I think we'll both feel better after we've eaten."

"I don't know," Finn said doubtfully. "I wonder if you're ever going to feel better about me. You see, I'm not sure I can change, Laurie. I'm not sure I can magically turn into somebody like Philip. I want to be perfect for you, but I honestly doubt that I can change that much."

"I know," Lauren said. Taking a deliberately candid attitude, she went on, "Neither of us should have to change, Finn. The tough part is going to be calling it quits if we find we're completely incompatible."

Finn winced, but his optimism was quick to return. "You know, Laurie," he said, "I think you had the right idea when you suggested we'd feel better on full stomachs. Let's go eat." He smiled, but for once Lauren didn't find his grin infectious.

chapter 12

THE RESTAURANT, IT turned out, was crowded and noisy, with a band that was already performing a set of beach-party sixties numbers so loud that the small lamp on the maître d's desk was vibrating with the thumping beat. Lauren hesitated just inside the doorway.

Finn seemed to know exactly what she was thinking. "Let's go across the hall," he said into her ear. He took her elbow cautiously and pulled her back out of the restaurant. "There's a sushi bar."

Lauren drew back out of instinctive revulsion. "That's raw fish!"

Finn grinned a little at her expression and insisted, propelling her down the lavishly decorated corridor to a smaller lobby. "Where's your sense of adventure?" he rebuked her. "Do you have a closed mind, after all?"

It was a challenge, of course, which Lauren had to accept or lose face. The cozy bar was an obscure niche tucked into the recesses of the large hotel, and it was not especially popular. The place was quiet and restfully attractive. Paper screens were illuminated from behind by oyster-white lights, and the small tables were decorated only with single flowers swimming in simple glass dishes. A casually dressed Japanese man greeted them.

In a moment, Lauren found herself in a small, intimate booth with Finn, who took up the menu and teased her by selecting just the items that sounded the worst: octopus, sea eel, yellowtail, sea urchin. When the waiter brought green tea, Lauren drank it with a thirst, anticipating that she wasn't going to be able to force herself to eat such awful things.

When the meal came soon thereafter, however, Lauren was pleasantly surprised by the pretty arrangement of colorful items presented to them on a plain wooden tray. Two dishes of aromatic sauces, one soy and the other a green mustard, were beautifully balanced by fingers of vinegared rice laced with a ribbon of dried seaweed and finally topped by delicate portions of surprisingly unrepulsive-looking fish. Thin ginger slices were provided to cleanse their palates between the various flavors.

Finn took up his chopsticks and was surprised that Lauren hadn't mastered the art. He showed her how to hold the sticks, practiced patiently with her, and finally, when Lauren became too flustered by his gentle attention to concentrate, he fed her this bite and that with a tender precision that made her inner dilemma even worse. How could one man be so many men?

The sushi was an aesthetic meal, one to be appreciated for the combination of color, texture, and the lovely simplicity of style as well as the delectable taste. The meal was a learning experience, one that Lauren was sure she would never forget—if not for the newness of the food, at least for the complexity of her partner. Halfway through the sushi, she found that her senses were once again coming alert to Finn. For the first time she was seeing him in a new atmosphere, one in which he was the leader and she was the less accomplished one. And she enjoyed it. She liked seeing Finn self-contained and experienced and—could it be true?—suave, without losing his genuine sensitivity. The evening was unique.

Lauren was very glad, and with increasingly frequent smiles and a steady regaining of her usual good spirits, she told him so.

They strolled around the hotel pool after that, listening to the music, but both admitted they were tired and finally walked back to their condominiums. Outside her door, Lauren turned to Finn and placed her hands on his arms.

"Good night, Finn," she said, tipping up to kiss him lightly on the mouth.

He didn't take her in his arms, but held her eyes with his. The question was obvious between them. They had made love before. Was the time right to do so again?

Finn did not press her, did not touch her. In a husky voice that hinted at his inner dismay, he abruptly asked, "Do you want me to go back to Washington?"

The question brought a hard lump to Lauren's throat. He was so easily wounded, so easily guilt-stricken. She moved and wrapped both arms around his body, hugging him swiftly. "No, Finn, I don't. I'm angry about the circumstances, but I'm happy with you here."

He kissed her then, his mouth as subtle and exciting as the unique meal they had just shared. Slowly, he gathered her up in his arms, holding her slim body close to his as he pressed his lips more firmly to her soon-trembling mouth. The tempo of his heartbeat accelerated against her breast, and Lauren felt a surge of emotion within herself. He was so sweet, and his quick response to her merest touch was so thrilling. Her own pulse pattered like the wings of an excited bird, and she instinctively molded her body to his.

As the sea breeze wrapped them in a cool moment of privacy and their mutual desire for each other became increasingly evident in all the subtle ways she had come to recognize, Lauren wondered distantly at her own fickle emotions. How could she be so furious and so in love with the same man in the span of just a few hours? How could she trust him so utterly one moment and then wonder at his actions the next? He was a chameleon, constantly changing, and Lauren wasn't sure she knew him sometimes.

There was too much to decide before she could allow

herself the pleasure of lying in his arms again. With regret, Lauren broke the kiss, though she remained just centimeters from his mouth for a split second, as if tantalized by the possibilities.

"I know," murmured Finn, having read her uncertainty in the way her embrace changed. He loosened her a fraction and said, "I'll see you in the morning, all right?"

"Oh, Finn," Lauren breathed. "Am I being an immature, unsophisticated fool all of a sudden?"

"No," said Finn, on a shaken laugh. "That's my territory, remember?"

"You don't have a corner on that market," Lauren said bitterly, giving him a final, hard kiss on his mouth. "Believe me! Good night."

"Good night, Lauren."

Lauren went back to her bedroom and flinched when she turned on the light. She stared at the bed, and wasn't surprised to find that her eyes were stinging. Sleeping alone tonight was not going to be very appealing at all. She got undressed and climbed in under the bedcovers, then proceeded to spend the night tossing and turning and dreaming of what might have happened in that bed had Finn shared it with her.

She woke early, and the sun was brilliant. Determined to enjoy herself, Lauren put on her bathing suit and a big straw hat and went out onto the beach with a large towel, a bottle of sun screen, and a thick paperback novel with a deliciously lurid cover. She rented a big beach umbrella and dragged it close to the lapping high tide before spreading out her paraphernalia. A day of baking in the sun—perfect.

Finn did not appear until almost eleven, and when he did, he gave Lauren a warm kiss that sent her heart out of control. A night of dreaming about his lovemaking had heightened her desire for him. The sunshine was hot on her thighs, and she gave him a quivery smile when he sat back on his heels to admire her bathing suit. He had no time for small talk, though, and before Lauren could ask him questions about his plans for the day, he was running off on some errand. Too amazed by her own vacillating feelings and suddenly too sun-lazed to follow, she decided to bask in the sun and let Finn go off on his own. Perhaps he needed time to think as much as she did.

At one o'clock, he reappeared with lunch. He'd been to a market and came with a bag of stone crab claws, which they took turns pounding open with the end of a knife. They ate on the beach, making a meal of the crab, two cold beers, and some fluffy baking-powder biscuits that they dipped into a jar of homemade strawberry preserves. They talked about what Finn had seen on the island, and then a young couple and their two preschool-aged children appeared on the beach with pails and shovels, and Finn was irresistibly drawn into helping with a sandcastle. He was carefully lining shells along the wall above the moat when Lauren fell asleep.

Later, after she woke up, they went for a swim and then took a walk up the beach, after which Lauren picked up her gear and went inside for a quick shower. She heard Finn moving around out on their shared patio and went out to join him, her hair still wet but combed slickly back from her face. He was having a look at a barbecue grill there.

"What's up?"

"Not dinner," Finn said, straightening to smile at her. "At least not yet. I got some stuff to cook, but now I'm not so sure I know how."

Lauren pulled a fearful face. "Not lobster that we have to kill ourselves or anything like that, I hope?"

Finn shook his head hastily. "The ladies at the fish market tried to sell me some lobsters, but I couldn't imagine cooking them. You have to dump them *live* into boiling water!"

Lauren laughed at him and hugged him then without thinking. He could be so dear sometimes. Then, briskly, she let him go, and went along with him to the kitchenette in his condo to lend a hand with dinner. They puttered together, with Lauren in command, and finally sautéed some shrimp with strips of vegetables and rice. They ate on the beach again, sitting in the sand and balancing their plates precariously. As a beverage they drank a very nice white wine that Finn had been chilling in the refrigerator of his kitchenette.

Afterward, they walked up the beach to a posh ice-cream parlor, where Lauren indulged her craving for chocolate with a huge scoop of Swiss chocolate almond.

They found a table outdoors under a striped awning, and the family at the next table greeted Finn excitedly.

"Who are they?" Lauren asked, when they finally sat down to enjoy their dessert.

"Some people I met at the grocery store this morning."

"You must have spent a long time there!" she said, laughing. "They seem to know you pretty well."

"I like going to the grocery," Finn told her, scraping the whipped cream off his strawberry sundae in one careful scoop. Then, savoring the taste and pulling the spoon out of his mouth upside down, he added, "Do you ever just watch the babies in a store? They're amazing. They're fascinated by all the color and the lights and the people. It's great just to see how they absorb all that stimulation without trying to make any sense out of it."

Lauren smiled. "You go shopping simply to watch babies?"

"The older kids are fun to watch, too. They pester their mothers for all the stuff they see advertised on television. I think they do it just to test their limits sometimes, you know?"

"Sounds like you enjoy observing people," Lauren suggested, licking at her ice cream.

"Sure. I take my time and wander aimlessly around. The little kids—three and four years old—are the most fun, because they're not too uptight or intimidated to stop and talk."

"You don't pass out lollipops, do you?"

He shook his head. "Never give candy to strange kids."

"You amaze me sometimes," Lauren said, putting both her elbows on the small table.

Finn shrugged. He looked uncomfortable suddenly, as if she had caught him admitting something that he thought ought to be kept secret. He stirred his ice cream but didn't eat it for a moment. He said, "Somebody once told me that hanging around grocery stores is my way of making social contact with people while still remaining anonymous. I'm antisocial."

Lauren put down her ice cream. "Who told you that?"

"Betsy. She's—"

"Oh," Lauren interrupted. She snatched up her cone again and said heavily, "Her."

Finn looked at Lauren in startled surprise. "What does that mean?"

"Nothing. I met her. I saw her, I mean."

"So?"

"So nothing."

Finn tipped his head. "Hey, I'm the one who's supposed to clam up when things get personal. What's the cool reaction all about?"

Lauren sighed. He had been right on the plane. She had needed some time to get a grip on her thoughts and feelings. She wasn't afraid of losing her temper and hurting Finn's feelings anymore, but the day had been so pleasant without having to talk about the trouble between them. It was with unwillingness that Lauren broke the ice. She avoided Finn's eyes and said, "I met Betsy on the stairs coming out of your apartment last weekend. I was coming out, that is. She was going in."

"Hmm," said Finn, and he went studiously back to eating his ice cream. "Sunday was a memorable morning, wasn't it?"

"Yes," Lauren said. "It was. Was Betsy the one who once told you that your priorities are sometimes skewed?"

"No, that was my wife."

Lauren gave up on her ice cream altogether. "Now that brings up yet another subject that interests me."

"Kimberly? We talked about her once."

"But we never got all the details out in the open. Finn, there's no sense in pretending that we—that you and I aren't interested in each other . . ."

Finn put down his spoon very carefully, and he wasn't able to look Lauren in the face. Cautiously, he asked, "Is this the right time to do this?"

"Talk? We've been putting it off a long time. I know

you're not comfortable baring your soul, Finn, but it seems silly to pretend that we haven't got a lot to say to each other." She watched his bent head for signs of reaction. Sometimes he could really be exasperating. Without thinking, she said, "Now please don't look like I've just forced cod-liver oil on you."

Finn's head snapped up. "Look, you've known all along that I'm not as well adjusted as Philip Bank and Trust. I'm sorry. I care about you and I'd like something good between us, but I'm just not capable of cutting myself open and letting my id come boiling out, Doctor. If you want to talk about Betsy and Kimberly, go ahead, but I'm not good at talking about me."

Lauren ignored his sarcasm and pounced quickly. "Are you afraid I'm not going to like what's inside of you?"

Finn seemed almost angry. Lauren sensed that he was almost on the brink of saying something quick and sharp, and that would have been a first. As always, though, he controlled the impulse. Lauren felt disappointment inside, for he had almost reacted naturally. His temper came and went as swiftly as all the other emotions that blew across his features, though, and once again, he was mild-mannered Finn Gallagher.

Whatever response he was trying to formulate for her never made it out of his head. A boy of about ten years had come sidling up to their table, and he tugged shyly at Finn's shirt.

Finn looked around at the boy in surprise.

"Hi," said the boy. "I'm Tim, remember? Want to see what I practiced?"

"Sure."

Tim began to fumble with a quarter, resting it on the back of his hand and clumsily flipping it between his fingers. He frowned and said, "I've almost got it."

"Looks good," Finn approved, smiling. He took the boy's hand and set the quarter in a slightly different spot. "Now try."

Tim tried the trick again, and this time it worked. The coin disappeared between his fingers briefly, then reap-

peared when he made a flourish at Finn's bent ear. His
parents cheered from the next table.

"Great!" Finn exclaimed, cheerfully whapping Tim on
his back. "You've got it!"

"Show me another trick," Tim begged.

Naturally, Finn obliged. He flipped the quarter in the air
and made a funny whistle, and when he caught the coin
again, there were two quarters in his palm. Magic. Tim was
delighted, and Finn set to work teaching him the trick. He
was patient, first demonstrating slowly, then manipulating
Tim's pudgy hands through the complex motions. With his
family looking on, the boy mastered the trick.

Lauren sat back and watched. She could have gotten
angry. She could have been disgusted with Finn for abandoning their heart-to-heart so abruptly, but there was no use
losing her temper. Finn was Finn, and there was going to
be no changing him.

The thought made her sad. Finn had his faults, and no
amount of Dr. Lauren Chambers's therapy was going to
make him perfect. He was a grown man, not a boy who
could be gently helped to mature into the perfect mate.
Finn's flaw was that he was never going to be able to devote
all of his attention to anything or anyone. He wasn't capable
of loving a woman above all else. He would always have
something on his mind—whether it was magic tricks for
little kids or computer programs for the Pentagon.

The people at other tables around them were soon watching and applauding as Tim learned more and more, and
finally someone called out for Finn to do a trick. He laughed
and shook his head, but in the next instant he pulled a pretty
paper rose from Tim's shirt pocket. The crowd applauded
and called for more, so Finn laid aside the rose and got up.

Lauren looked at the flower. It was the one he had tried
to give her on the airplane, and now he was pleasing a mob
of strangers with it. She picked it up unconsciously and got
to her feet. When she looked back, Finn was getting ready
to pull a tablecloth out from under a full load of dishes and
glassware. The ice-cream-shop patrons were all calling out

words of encouragement, and some were standing up to watch the feat. Finn was the center of attention, gladly pleasing a roomful of strangers.

Lauren went out into the twilight and walked away. Twirling the paper rose in her hands, she walked down to the beach alone.

chapter 13

"LAUREN!"

She had been walking slowly, but in ten minutes she must have walked far out of sight of the ice cream shop. Somehow Finn had known where to look for her. She stopped and waited for him at the edge of the water, where the surf washed almost to her bare toes before receding quietly.

A shamefaced Finn was slow in coming to her side.

Before he could speak, Lauren said, "Don't say it, all right?"

"I'm sorry?"

She nodded and turned to put her face to the open sea. Her throat hurt, and she didn't want him to see how close she was to tears. "That seems to be the way you and I open conversations now."

"Okay," said Finn, taking her arm. He turned her so that they could continue walking up the beach. "I'm *not* sorry, to tell you the truth."

Lauren glanced up. "This is new."

"No, it's not. It's old, in fact. Thirty-one years. Lauren,"

Finn said simply, "it's the way I am. I'm not like all your other boyfriends. You've probably got a hundred all at the same time, I know, but I'm the one you've decided to fall in love with."

Lauren stopped dead and looked up in astonishment. "Finn!"

"Don't deny it," he said quickly, facing her. He rushed ahead before she could speak. "I can see you're in love with me as much as I'm crazy about you. It's not so amazing, so don't look as though I've just given you cod-liver oil."

For once Finn was not lost and puzzled or confused and hurt. He wasn't exactly calm and collected either, though. His dark eyes were full of shadows, and his grip on her arm was sure and hard. "Look, I don't know what's gotten you interested in me in the first place, but I'm glad you *are* interested. I love you, Lauren. I really do. I want to be with you, but you've taken it into your head that we're somehow not suited for each other. You've been looking for an excuse never to see me again since we first met."

"I have not!"

"Haven't you? What's all this junk about Betsy, then?"

Lauren yanked out of his grasp. "Junk? You tell me! You've practically got her living on your doorstep!"

"She lives downstairs, for godsake!"

"What's she doing coming up to your apartment before breakfast on a Sunday morning?"

"You're jealous of Betsy!" Finn cried out in amazement. "I don't believe it!"

"Darn right I'm jealous!"

"Lauren," he said patiently, "For crying out loud, she's just a friend. She came to talk, that's all. You've got friends of the opposite sex, I know you have."

"Not ones who come waltzing into my apartment at all hours of the day and night."

"She didn't waltz in. The door was locked."

"But you let her in, right? Even if she'd come an hour earlier, you'd have gone and opened the door."

"What do you mean?"

"I mean," Lauren said bluntly, "that if the phone had

rung or somebody had knocked on your door while we were in the middle of—of—well, if we were busy, you would have gotten out of bed to answer it!"

Finn threw up his hands. "People need me sometimes!"

"*I* need you sometimes!" Lauren shouted, losing control. She was sad and angry and feeling desperate.

Gently, quickly, Finn said, "I wouldn't have answered the door if we were making love."

"Thanks," Lauren snapped, turning away from him before he saw how upset she was. "But you're going to have to prove it to me sometime."

Finn caught up with her half an instant later. He didn't touch her arm, but shoved his hands down into his trouser pockets as he walked. "Lauren, this is too heavy for me to understand all at once. Let's take it slow, all right? I'm a quick study, but this soul-searching of yours is tough."

"What are you talking about?"

Finn sighed and kept pace with her. "We're talking about you and me now, aren't we? Not Betsy or Kimberly or Philip or anyone else. You and me."

"I guess so," Lauren said steadily. "I'm waiting for your usual diversion before I really get down to the nitty-gritty, so—"

"Diversion?" he interrupted.

Lauren looked up. "You're not running away as you usually do. As soon as I start expressing my feelings, are you going to find a diversion?"

"I don't get it."

"You know what I mean. When things start getting— well, intimate, you immediately change the subject or find an excuse to leave me."

"I do not!"

"You just did it fifteen minutes ago," Lauren said firmly. She stopped walking and faced him. "We were calmly getting to a few issues that have been bothering me, and you seized the first chance that came along to—"

"All right," said Finn. "You're right. I'm not good at getting in touch with my feelings. I'm uncomfortable."

"You're uncomfortable? Look, I spent the night with

you, remember? I made love with you, and when you went gleefully back to your computer to plan the next attack on the planet Mars, I found myself completely forgotten. Don't you think that made *me* feel a little uncomfortable? I walked out!"

"And you met Betsy on the steps," Finn guessed. "That made things even worse in your mind."

"In my *mind?*" she demanded. She turned away and folded her arms across her chest to quiet her pounding heart and took two deep breaths, trying to calm down. Over her shoulder, she said, "Don't you start second-guessing what's going on in my mind, Finn Gallagher. I'm a psychologist, don't forget!"

"How could I forget it?" Finn asked bitterly. "You throw your profession in my face twice every hour."

Lauren spun around. "What does that mean?"

Finn spread his hands, palms up. "You're analyzing all the time. You're looking for what makes people tick. You're cool and quiet, always watching what I do and say, and you get this cold, scary look in your eyes, as if I were a white mouse you'd like to dissect! For Pete's sake, Lauren, can't you relax and take me at face value?"

Lauren stared up at him speechlessly.

"I'm a nice guy," Finn went on in a rush to explain himself. "But I'm not going to go into the nearest phone booth and change into my Superman outfit. I'm always Clark Kent, Lauren! I'm not very adept with people, I'm preoccupied with my work, I'll grant you, and I'm a little dull. That's me! That's the way I am!"

"You're not dull," Lauren said stiffly.

"Thank you. You're not, either."

"You *are* preoccupied with your work, however," she added. "And that bugs me."

He nodded. "I could use some help in that area, I admit. I'm not capable of giving absolute, undivided devotion, though. That's been obvious, hasn't it? If that's what you want—"

"I'll get a dog," Lauren finished sharply.

"Then you understand?" Finn asked ruthlessly. "I'm not

going to give you a fantasy-perfect love affair. I've got my own life to cope with, Lauren, and you've got yours. It would be nice to have an expert help me get a better balance between my personal and business life—"

Lauren glared at him. "I don't want to be your therapist!"

"Good. I don't want to be your client, either. Lauren, I love you."

She didn't respond. She met his eyes, though, and wondered for the briefest moment if he was in fact trying to convince himself that the words were true.

"Dammit!" Finn burst out, losing his temper as soon as he saw the flicker of doubt in her gaze. "Stop looking as if you think I don't know what love is!"

"Do you?" Lauren challenged him.

He was angry then. He spun away, took two fast paces to put some distance between them, and wheeled back on her. His voice was hard as he explained, "I'm not a kid anymore. I was married, and I know I was to blame for the failure of the marriage. I blew it with Kimberly, but not because I didn't love her. Do you want to analyze my marriage to find out if I'm capable of—"

"No, I don't want to talk about your marriage," Lauren interrupted hastily. "Especially if you still care for her."

"Care for—? For crying out loud!"

"Are you still married?"

Finn tried to laugh, but he was too astonished. "Is that what's upset you?"

"How am I supposed to know these things unless you tell me?" she cried.

Finn took a breath and said with forced calm, "Lauren, Kimberly and I got divorced at least eight years ago and I've never seen her since! Yes, I loved her once, and I still remember what it was like to want to know every minute where she was and what she was doing, but I've long since stopped caring for Kimberly. I feel that way about you, Lauren, only it's stronger. It's not just sex with you and me, it's a hundred other ways you touch me."

"Why? Why me, Finn?" Lauren demanded, her voice cracking and going too high. "What in the world attracted you to me of all the women in your life? You've got an apartment house full of them, and Steve tells me that there's been a steady parade of—"

"Don't listen to Steve," Finn said, making a swift gesture of annoyance. "Please! He's furious with me more than half the time for the things I ask him to do, no matter what I pay him. He's got—oh, hell, if you've been listening to him, I'm dead, aren't I?"

"That depends," Lauren muttered, looking up at Finn suspiciously. "Steve told me some very infuriating things about you."

"Well, forget them. Lauren, he must have seen the way I care for you. He knows he's out of a job if you become a permanent part of my life and I—"

"Oh, Finn—"

"Don't stop me," he said just as quickly, making a grab for her hand. "Lauren, I want you with me all the time. I can't get you out of my head, and when we're together, I feel so terrific I think my whole body's going to burst! And once in a while you get the prettiest soft look in your eyes, so I know you can't be unaffected by what's happened between us—"

"But why me, Finn?" Lauren repeated, shaking her head in amazement. "I don't know why you've picked me and done everything but stand on your head to impress me!"

"Because," Finn said earnestly, "you're like me inside. You enjoy things and take pleasure in just plain living! I think you're hiding the real Laurie Chambers from the rest of the world. I saw her the first time we met."

"One encounter on a streetcorner and you think—"

"Yes," Finn interrupted firmly. "When we ran into each other you weren't thinking about how the austere Dr. Chambers ought to be acting. That moment was fun and silly and we both loved it. Ever since then you've been trying to erase my memory of the expression in your face, the light that came into your eyes. When I went up to your office that night, I wondered if you were the same woman or her stuffy twin sister!"

"I am not stuffy."

"I know that. Laurie, you and I are basically the same kind of person—spontaneous but hardworking when the time comes. You're just trying so damn hard to change your mental image of yourself so that men like the stuffed shirt from the bank will accept you."

"Wait a minute!" Lauren ordered. "Are you suggesting that I'm pretending to be something I'm not?"

"Exactly."

"That's rich!" Lauren cried, and she pivoted on her heel, afraid she was going to lose her temper then. Striding angrily away from Finn along the shoreline, she shouted to the wind, "Which one of us has been through more costume changes than Barnum and Bailey?"

"I'm still me on the inside!" Finn claimed, calling after her. "You've been wearing the same old dress-for-success suits for so long you're starting to lose all that sparkle inside."

Walking ahead of him, Lauren muttered, "Sparkle! He wants a woman with *sparkle!* He's got enough crazy fireworks inside to—oh, curses!" she shouted to the sky.

Down the beach, Finn called, "Now which one of us is running away?"

Lauren faced him, fifteen yards from the spot where he had halted. "I am not running away. I'm trying not to lose my temper and belt you, that's all."

"See?" Finn asked in delight. "If you didn't jam all that emotional stuff inside and cork it, you'd feel—"

"Don't lecture me about my feelings!"

"I've been honest with you from the start," Finn shouted. "I care for you, and I want to be with you. I want to make you happy."

"I *am* happy! When I'm with you I'm deliriously happy— at least during the times I'm not tempted to smack some sense into you!"

"Isn't it great?"

Lauren halted on the beach and whirled around in amazement. "Great?!"

"Yes!" He laughed. "We love each other!"

"I've loved somebody before, Finn, and we both know

that love alone doesn't make everything wonderful!"

"We can do it," he insisted, still several yards away.

"Can we? *We?* Or me? Is one of us going to have to do all the hard work to maintain a good relationship?"

He made a disgusted face. "You're talking like the doctor now."

"I *am* a doctor! I'm an expert at this, remember?"

"You're an expert with other people's marriages. Analyzing a situation doesn't fix it. You can't diagnose the disease to make it stop."

"Are you lecturing me on how to keep a marriage afloat?" Lauren demanded.

"I guess I am," Finn said steadily, and he came to stand in front of her, hands still safely in his pockets. "I've been there before, remember?"

"I've been close, too."

"And you blew it. One or both of you did." Cautiously, Finn reached for her and passed a soft caress up Lauren's arm. He didn't meet her eyes for a moment, but smiled just a little. "If we pool what we already know, Laurie, we might have a shot at a very nice marriage."

"Marriage?" Lauren repeated, her voice sounding odd as he stroked her arm gently and took possession of her wrist. "I thought we were discussing a relationship here."

"What's the difference?"

"Finn!"

"What?" he asked with a smile, pulling her body close to his own.

"Are you—" Lauren gulped back a dozen different emotions. "Do you expect me—after—how can I—oh, blast!"

Lauren gave up trying to make any sense. She yanked free of Finn and flung herself away from him in exasperation.

"Lauren," Finn called when she turned away and started marching up the beach. He was laughing again. "Lauren, wait!"

She didn't. Too many thoughts and emotions were boiling inside, and Lauren had to work off the tension. She strode rapidly up the hard-packed sand at the water's edge.

"Lauren," Finn said again, close behind her and breathless with laughter as well as exertion. "Darling—"

Glancing ahead, Lauren saw something that made her freeze in midstride, her breath caught in her throat in a gasp. Finn collided with her from behind, wrapping his arms automatically around her. "Lauren, you're—what's wrong?" He tightened his embrace and followed her straining eyes up the beach.

"What is that?" Lauren asked, her voice taut and high.

There was a lump on the sand just a few yards ahead of them. Too large for a sand crab, too small for an adult human body. In the half-light, her first reaction had been fear, of course. The beach was far from the lights of the hotel, and the breeze was suddenly eerie around them. Lauren shrank instinctively against Finn.

He pointed. "Look. Somebody's running away."

He was right. Two, no, three figures were disappearing into the scrub trees above them, running away from the abandoned thing on the sand. Finn cautiously stepped around Lauren and put himself between her and whatever lay before them. He kept his voice light. "Don't panic. It's not a person, look. And it's dead, whatever it is."

"Is it a dolphin?"

"No, no," Finn replied immediately, still peering through the darkness to make out the shape. In surprise, he said, "It's a sea turtle. On its back. Look."

"Oh, how sad," Lauren breathed shakily.

"Are you all right?" he asked, cupping her shoulders with returning gentleness and looking down at her once more.

"Just scared for a second," she admitted, trying to sound brave. She remained against him, though, glad that Finn felt so warm and strong just then. She did not try to look over his shoulder at the dead turtle. She shivered. "I thought—it looked like a body when I first saw it."

Finn turned her gently, heading them both back toward the lights and their condominiums. His arm was around her body, his hand riding lightly along her ribs. He said, "Your heart's going crazy. Do you want to sit down for a second?"

She shuddered again. "No, no, let's go back."

"Right," said Finn, and he led her a few steps back down the beach. Then he let her go long enough to strip off his jacket. Wrapping it around her shoulders, he was gentle once more, taking charge and handling her deftly. His head was close to hers. His hands slowed and finally rested under her arms momentarily. He eased closer. "Lauren..."

It was easy to melt into his arms. Lauren leaned against his body and let him gather her up in a warmly comforting, then increasingly exhilarating embrace. She closed her eyes and lifted her face to his. Finn kissed her softly once, and then he took a long, long breath and bent once more to kiss her thoroughly. He wound one arm around her body and used his other hand to hold her head, to caress her cheek, to memorize the curve of her face with his fingertips. Lauren's head began to swim with images—the soft caress of the sea-tinged air and the subtle scent of Finn and the beach around them. His body was secure and vibrant, and she wrapped her arms unsteadily around his neck.

The moment might have been an eternity. Lauren's heart swelled until it hurt inside her, and still she couldn't hold him tightly enough. When Finn eased away and nuzzled her throat, kissing her lightly here and there, she heard her voice say his name unsteadily, time and again.

Finally, she became aware that his quick, communicative kisses had ceased. She lifted her head, and saw his expression clouding.

"Finn, what is it?"

He was in the act of casting a glance over his shoulder, but at her words, he snapped his attention down to her. "What?"

He was miles away again! He was looking at her, but with a vacant stare, as if the kisses of an instant ago had never happened. "What's in your head right now?" she demanded.

"Now?" he asked blankly. He let her go and began backing away, looking apologetic. "Forgive me. I wasn't listening, but not because I don't love you. I was—look, it will just take a second, I promise. Stay here and I'll—"

"Where are you going?" Lauren demanded, staring at him in amazement.

"If it's still alive, I'll never forgive myself for walking away," Finn said quickly, backing up the beach again. "I just want to make sure. Wait here. I have to check."

"Finn," Lauren began in exasperation.

But he was off again. He had been holding her, kissing her, telling her that he loved her, and at the same time thinking about that cursed turtle! The man was uncanny! Lauren stood still and watched him go, shaking her head. He was swift and graceful in the rising moonlight, trotting back to the turtle and carefully, gently, bending down on one knee beside it. He put out a cautious hand and touched the thing. Lauren knew how that touch might feel. Finn was sensitive and careful, tentative perhaps at first, but his confidence would grow and he might give the thing a small, tender caress.

He got up and spun around in one quick, excited move. "It's alive!"

"Oh, Finn!" Lauren took two steps. Her tumultuous emotions drained away, as if washed by a cleansing wave of the ocean. Looking from the turtle to Finn and back, she asked breathlessly, "Are you sure?"

"Somebody's turned her over on her back," he said in a rush, moving around the turtle's body to check for injuries. "Probably those kids who ran off. She'll drown when the tide comes in before she can roll over by herself."

Lauren arrived at the turtle again. "What can we do?"

"Flip her over, I guess. Can you—"

"It's awfully big," Lauren observed doubtfully. In her mind, a reptile was still a reptile, and this turtle was not nearly as cute as the ones pictured in children's books. It was darned ugly, in fact—not at all like the smiling character that won the race against the storybook rabbit—and Lauren looked down at the poor beached creature with mixed emotions. Grabbing hold of the thing was not something she wanted to do without some forethought.

Finn was already kicking off his shoes so he could get a better footing in the sand. He rolled up one shirtsleeve and then the other. "She probably weighs less than a hundred pounds. It shouldn't be too tough. We'd better hurry. The tide's already washing up this far."

He was correct, of course. The surf wasn't high, but each successive wash of foamy seawater came farther under the curved shell of the turtle. Well, there wasn't enough time to run back to the hotel for reinforcements, and it looked as though Finn was ready to start the rescue this very minute. With a steadying breath to gather courage, Lauren laid her shoes on the sand and put Finn's folded jacket on top of them. Hitching up her skirt, she knelt in the sand on the opposite side of the turtle from Finn. "Tell me what to do."

"Don't look so sick," he said lightly, and he grinned at her with a glimmer of kindness in his dark eyes. "You can stand back, if you like. I think I can do it, if you're squeamish."

"Nonsense," Lauren said firmly, though when she laid her hand on the turtle's shell, she was shaking.

"Okay," Finn said. "If you can steady her on that side, I'll push from here. We'll set her on her feet where you are now, so get ready to jump."

"Count on me, coach," Lauren cracked. "I know how to get out of the way."

"Ready?" he asked, crouching beside the turtle. He got a grip and started to push.

"All set," she replied. She watched as Finn heaved. The turtle began to roll up on the edge of its shell, and she called softly, "Easy, Finn. Its legs on this side are going to get squished in the sand. Careful."

The turtle flapped her foot then, and Lauren squeaked, startled. Finn laughed, sounding breathless, and the sand shifted. He blew a noisy sigh and gave up, putting the turtle back down just where she had been in the first place.

"Too heavy?" Lauren asked anxiously.

"Too clumsy," Finn corrected, frowning now as he looked the creature over once more. "I can't get a grip on her."

"I think it's going to get hurt when you flip it," Lauren said, laying both her hands on the turtle's belly as if to comfort it. "I thought turtles could pull in all their legs."

"This is a *big* turtle," Finn said, mocking his own inability to budge the thing.

"Let me help push," Lauren said quickly, and she got up, dusting the sand from her knees out of habit. She skirted the turtle, splashing through the surf to get to Finn's side. "If we both shove——"

"Good girl," he said. "You take her head. She's heavier at the other end. Ready?"

Beside him on the sand, Lauren dug in and prepared to shove. Her shoulder bumped Finn's. "Ready. On three?"

He nodded.

"One, two, three!"

They both pushed and grunted and the turtle wriggled once in dismay, and then with a shout of triumph from Finn, they heaved the creature over onto her belly. Finn took a gigantic step over it, steadying the turtle lest it get too much of a jolt, and he eased it down onto the sand.

"Wonderful!" Lauren cried, clapping her hands. "Is she all right?"

"Wait and see," Finn said tensely, watching. "Come on, old girl!"

The turtle must have known Finn meant no harm, for it turned toward him and made a clumsy about-face. It headed for the water then, and Finn got to his feet, watching it go with a delighted grin.

Crouched on the sand below him, Lauren looked up, observing the pleasure on his features and the proud way his hands rested on his trim hips. He had never seemed so full of life, so keenly unique and wonderfully handsome, as in that moment. The moonlight sparkled on the wild curliness of his hair, and his eyes were as dark and deep with turbulence as the ocean that lay before them.

As the turtle made its final escape into the sea, Lauren watched Finn a moment longer and finally said the words that came unbidden from her heart. "I love you, Finn Gallagher."

chapter 14

WASN'T HE A darling? Over the next several weeks, Lauren found herself asking that mental question a dozen times a day. It wasn't just Finn's exuberance for life that she loved, but his unfailing ability to, yes, to prioritize his life. Some things were just more important to Finn than others, and providing help seemed to be his specialty. Finn was always helping somebody, she discovered, and his biggest client was Lauren herself. He had rescued her from a very boring existence and brought her to a place where everything was constantly changing.

When she heard his voice in the outer office one Tuesday morning, Lauren switched off her dictating machine and smiled at the picture on her desk. It was Finn's face, eyes popped wide in delight and a big smile on his mouth. She had taken the picture herself.

He burst through the office door half a minute later. "Lauren, you've got to come upstairs!"

Folding her hands in her lap, she gave him a bemused smile. He wore his scruffy jeans and a hastily donned sweat

173

shirt that read SARAH LAWRENCE. His sneakers were sound-less on the carpet as he crossed to her desk with his usual energy. Lauren said, "Good morning, darling. Did the carpenters wake you? Tearing out another wall, are they?"

Finn grabbed her hand and hauled her to her feet. "They're putting in new windows. I can't stand windows that don't open, so we're changing them. Will you come up? Billy says you're free for two hours. Please?"

"How can I refuse?" she asked, laughing. "Won't you at least say good morning?"

Finn's grin was a mile wide as he pulled her across the office. "In the elevator," he promised. "I don't want to shock Billy."

At his desk, ears firmly plugged with the Dictaphone headset, Billy drawled, "Nothing shocks me anymore. Be back here by one o'clock, Doctor."

Lauren saluted in the last instant before Finn dragged her out into the hall. "Finn, for heaven's sake, won't you give me a hint? What's all this about?"

"You won't believe it," he said, punching the elevator button. "It's so amazing that you've got to see it. Oh, and the furniture was delivered. Looks great. The decorator comes this afternoon, I think, to organize everything. Good morning, love."

He gathered her up then with his usual style, quick without being rough, skillful without being too practiced. His embrace still felt joyously new, even after a whole month of living together. Lauren wound her arms around his shoulders and when the elevator took that swift, upward surge, she felt her spirit give an extra leap.

Finn smiled and pressed his nose to hers, so that they were happily eye to eye. His voice dropped to a murmur. "I'm sorry I didn't say it properly this morning. I love you. Good morning."

Lauren kissed him back, sighing with the pleasure of his mouth on hers, his arms so snug around her body. She held him hard, sliding her hands up into the curling thickness of his hair. She fit her hips neatly against his lean frame, melting erotically, teasingly, to him. Finn always responded to her with passion, and this morning was no different. His arms tightened, he slanted his head to take her mouth more completely with his, and he gently pulled her body into alignment with his own, laughing softly as he did so.

The elevator doors parted then, and reluctantly Lauren remembered the time and place. She loosened Finn's grip and smiled into his eyes. "I love mornings with you. They last all day."

"And night," he said softly, running one hand down the curve of her waist. "Lauren . . ."

"No, you animal," she teased him, fighting her way out of his arms to lead him into the penthouse. "Not now and certainly not in the elevator. The carpenters must already think we're newlyweds after all the scenes they've interrupted."

"They've gone out for lunch," Finn argued, though he didn't protest when Lauren led him by the hand. "They wouldn't interrupt this time."

Failing to hide her smile, Lauren sent a wryly inquiring glance up at him. "Did you send them out again?"

He grinned and lifted his shoulders. "They promised to stay out until one, as long as I pick up the tab for lunch and don't tell their boss."

"You're impossible!" Lauren cried in reprimand. "How do you expect them to finish this place if you keep sending them out so we can—"

"They're almost finished now," Finn interrupted smoothly. "See? What do you think?"

They had commandeered the top floor of the downtown building, and now the penthouse was nearly finished. The carpenters had ripped out walls to make the space wide open and full of light. The staid office-building windows had been exchanged for floor-to-ceiling panes that allowed the panoramic view of Baltimore and the harbor, of course, into the living room. The effect was airy and spacious, but it was going to take a decorator's magic combined with all the paraphernalia that both Lauren and Finn had brought to their new living quarters to make the place look homey. So far, what the penthouse lacked in character, it made up in chaos. The rubble of the carpenters clashed with the elegant furniture that had been just delivered.

Only the huge sectional sofa was in place, looking like a graceful serpent as it wound around the open-pit fireplace and the new, curving wall that led into the kitchen. The rest of the furniture—mostly modern pieces upholstered in lovely pastels and a few glass-topped tables to match—had been cautiously placed out of the way of the builder's tools.

The final project was to install an arched greenhouse roof over a section of the balcony to make it an all-season room for who-knew-what purpose. Finn had liked the idea, so there it was. He had taken days to come up with the plans for renovating the top floor of the office building, and then he had given all his ideas to an architect who scratched his head and said he wasn't sure it was possible, but he'd give it a try. Within a week, though, the place had been under construction.

"What do you think?" Finn asked.

"The furniture? Lovely. You *did* say that somebody was going to come arrange it, right? I don't know if I'm capable of a project like this, Finn."

"The decorator will take care of everything, I promise. I don't have time to do it, and neither do you. The dining-room table didn't come, by the way. We've got another week's wait for that."

"The store has done a remarkable job in what little time they had," Lauren observed. "My love, how do you manage to make everything happen so fast? I wait two weeks for a hair-styling appointment, and you've accomplished so much here!"

"Now you know why I never get haircuts," Finn said with a grin. "Come on. Lunch is this way."

He took her by the hand through the hallway and back to the opposite end of the penthouse, the rooms that had been completed first and no longer had layers of dust and piles of lumber in them. A huge bathroom with a Jacuzzi that they hadn't had time to try out yet, Finn's computer lab where he was already creating such a clutter that Lauren was afraid to set foot inside for fear she'd ruin the next project for the Pentagon and cause World War III, and Lauren's study, a soundproof room with quiet stacks of books and a big leather chair for curling up. Their bedroom lay at the back, and Finn drew her there.

"What are you planning?" Lauren asked suspiciously when he drew her inside the quiet of their room and closed the door. He hadn't made the bed, she observed, and the billowing white curtains were still drawn against the morning sunshine. "Finn, is there really lunch here for me, or are you—"

"There's one great advantage to not having a dining-room table yet," Finn said, pulling her to the bed.

"Are those sandwiches?" Lauren asked, kicking off her shoes. "I apologize, darling. You're not an animal, after all."

"Don't make hasty judgments. Ham and cheese?"

"Orange soda, too?"

"Yep. No wine on a Tuesday. You're still on duty, Doctor."

They climbed into the heaps of pillows, and Lauren plumped one up especially to make Finn comfortable. She touched a kiss to his mouth and said, "You're so nice to me. I never had such good care before."

Finn smiled and forgot lunch, gathering her up in his arms easily. "That goes two ways. I thought you'd be disgusted about last night."

"That you didn't come to bed? I'm getting used to your hours. Was it four when you finally showed up here?"

"I think so. Did I wake you?"

"By kissing the back of my neck and curling up to get warm? By putting those freezing cold hands of yours on—"

"I'm sorry," Finn begged, laughing with her. "I won't do it again, I promise."

"Not until tonight, that is," Lauren retorted with a grin. "I don't mind, honestly. I'm glad that at least you finally did come to bed, to tell you the truth. Did you finish your project?"

"All done," he assured her, easing her down into the

pillows so they were more comfortably nestled together. "Jerry's going to call later with something new, though. And it's probably time for another emergency with DataBak, so I'll have to clear the decks for that."

"One emergency after another," Lauren said with a sigh.

"You have them, too," Finn pointed out calmly. "It was *your* client who called at nine on Saturday night."

"Touché," Lauren agreed, and she stretched her arms before wrapping them around his shoulders. Still smiling, she asked, "Do you mind, Finn? We're not exactly living like an ordinary couple, you know. Is this arrangement working out the way you expected?"

"I'm not going to back out," he said promptly, and he gave her a kiss on the mouth to silence her. "It's going to work, Laurie. I promise. It'll be fun."

"It's fun, but it's exhausting sometimes."

"Then we'll take the boat and go out for a while. There's no need to get overwhelmed by everything that happens."

Lauren held back a sigh and looked into his eyes. "You're very busy," she said seriously. "I didn't know how busy until we started living here, Finn. It scares me sometimes. You work so hard."

"Then we'll ease things down," he vowed quietly, nibbling at her earlobe. "I want to take time to enjoy being with you, Laurie."

Lauren stroked his face and watched his dark eyes for a moment. Though there were still fears in her mind about the mundane logistics of such a relationship, she was coming to the realization that she wouldn't have her life any other way. Being with Finn like this was a unique pleasure, too wonderful, too remarkable to let go. She whispered, "I'm glad. I love you, Finn. I love being with you. I've never known a man who could care so deeply about everything."

Their kiss was slower this time, more leisurely and thorough. Finn rolled Lauren gently on her back and lay on his elbows above her, all the while savoring her mouth, exploring the contour of her lips with his tongue. His hair felt wild but soft in her fingers, and his shoulders were strong beneath her hands. Lauren absorbed a small quiver of excitement as she laid her palms against Finn's chest, and while smiling against his mouth, she began to loosen the tie on his sweat shirt.

She tugged at it, and Finn laughed. He broke the kiss at her unspoken message and said, "I thought you were only interested in lunch."

"Since you don't come to bed at night, and I get up early every morning," Lauren responded with a prim smile, "lunch is beginning to have a totally different connotation in my life."

Finn smiled. He didn't need to answer. He began to unbutton her dress with gentle hands, and ducked obediently out of his shirt when Lauren pulled it over his head. With fleeting kisses and laughter, they undressed each other. In moments, they rolled together on the bed, bare limbs tangling with delicious familiarity now. Lauren stroked Finn's strong back and smiled languidly with him. She loved the way he held her so gently yet so purposefully, his hands sensitive to her slightest change of mood, it seemed. He was perfect.

"There," murmured Finn. "That's the look I love. Like you'd trust me for anything."

"Yes," Lauren responded, pressing a kiss to his mouth. "I do. Finn, make love with me."

He slipped his hand between her knees and smoothed his way up the tender flesh of her inner thigh. Lauren quivered at the swiftness of his caress. He knew just which touches gave her the most pleasure, which caresses should be slow and which ones sent her tumbling into desire. Just the same, she remembered each nuance of motion, each of Finn's responses to her slightest action so that together they made beautiful, sometimes shattering love. He said in relief, "And I was worried that I couldn't wait until dessert! Laurie, love, you feel so perfect, so warm and womanly."

She knew he wanted her quickly, with the exuberance of daylight. She pulled his head to her breast and held him gently there while she explored his body. She teased him, increasing his desire with small caresses and softly whispered words. Her own excitement came quickly, for Finn coaxed her body with tiny kisses and the intimate touches that he knew set her afire.

At last Lauren drew him against her body and within. Their joining was swift, but for a long while they lay quietly together, communing as one in a timeless embrace. When Finn moved inside her, he was slow and languid, bringing her to a peak of delight and watching while her eyes widened briefly and then closed in an unconscious surrender to her inner sensations. Her moment of fulfillment came too soon, almost, and Lauren wrapped her arms around Finn to hold him still. She had never known such quiet pleasure, it seemed, though each time they made love, it was better than the last.

Finn murmured her name, and Lauren opened her eyes. She kissed him then, holding his head between her hands. With her thighs still clasped around his hips, she pushed, rolling him over onto his back. Once above him, Lauren sought to bring Finn the same wondrous pleasure he had given her moments before. He wriggled once and laughed when she teased him, but then the urgency boiled over and he pulled her down to his chest for the final, ferocious thrusts that brought an unconscious groan from deep inside him.

Lauren stroked his hair from his face, not surprised to find the curls were damp against her fingers. She kissed him lightly on the temple.

"Don't go," he begged her some time later when she shifted her weight imperceptibly. "You're not hungry yet, are you?"

"My thoughts couldn't be further from food," Lauren said softly. "Oh, Finn."

"Happy?" he asked, his voice as quiet as hers.

"Yes, very." Lauren snuggled against his throat and said, "I want to make you happy, too, Finn. Anything that would please you, I'd do in a minute."

"How about next week?" he asked.

Lauren recognized his playful tone, and she sat up a little to see his face. "What about next week?"

Finn smiled lazily. "You said anything. How about marrying me?"

"Oh, Finn—"

"I said it wrong," he corrected hastily, catching her hair in his hands to hold her firmly above him. "Lauren, my love, will you marry me? Next week? After the greenhouse is finished?"

Lauren laughed. "Is that silly greenhouse the only thing that's keeping us from the altar? Yes, of course, I'll marry you next week. I'd do it sooner, you know."

"It'll take a week to get the penthouse finished for a wedding. And the guests of honor won't be back until then."

Lauren sat up for real then, her curiosity sparked by the laughter in Finn's eyes. "Who—what guests of honor?"

"You won't believe it," confided Finn, and he rolled over and reached for the night table. "Something came in this morning's mail. You'd better have a look."

Lauren pulled the bed sheet up into her lap and accepted the card from his hands. She read the signature first and cried, "Finn!"

"It's from Philip," Finn said calmly, though his grin was wide. "And Sally."

"Good grief! I don't believe it! 'We give up. Don't play any more tricks! Eloping today. Philip and Sally.' Finn!"

"How about that?" Finn demanded. "Chalk up another success to Interface! One more couple successfully set on a course of true love!"

"This is amazing!" Lauren cried. "How did they—wait a minute. What does this mean?" She pointed at the card in her hand. "'We give up. Don't play any more tricks.'"

Finn snatched the card from her and said quickly, "Don't pay any attention to that. It's nothing. What do you think? They're getting married!"

"Finn," Lauren said severely, "you've been tinkering with your computer again, haven't you? What have you done to poor Philip this time?"

"Nothing that he doesn't appreciate now," Finn countered. "Look, they're getting married. Aren't you happy?"

"They probably got married just to stop whatever you're doing to them! Tell me the truth, Finn. Did you lock them in a vault again?"

"No," Finn said contritely. "Nothing serious."

"Tell me!" she ordered, making a grab for his hair.

Finn ducked, but chose to obey. "I rigged it so they both were called for city tax audits on the same day. Nothing terrible, right?"

"Tax audits!"

"Harmless," Finn assured her. "I checked the computer records of both their accountants first. It's okay. They've run off to Nassau again, see? Check the postmark."

"You're amazing," Lauren said. "Absolutely amazing. You're not going to give up the matchmaking business, are you?"

"Why should I?" Finn asked smugly, and he gathered an unresisting Lauren in his arms again. "I'm having great financial success, there are hundreds of happy couples because of Interface, and even a well-known family therapist has given my company her seal of approval. Of course I'm not going to give it up!"

"I did not give my seal of approval," Lauren cried. "I simply—"

"Your article for the Sunday newspaper was a glowing description of the services Interface provides. You even told the whole city that you had found the man of your dreams through my computer service."

"Finding you had nothing to do with your computers," Lauren said quickly. "I didn't fall in love with you because of sheets of information provided by your company."

Finn hugged her hard, as if squeezing the argument out of her. "All right, all right. You promised to lend your expertise in perfecting the company, though, right? If Interface has an element you don't like, you're going to help me change it."

"Yes," Lauren agreed, molding her body to his once more. "I did promise that. You can call it my wedding present to you, all right?"

Finn laughed. "Wedding present? What am I going to give you?"

Lauren lifted her nose whimsically.

"Uh-oh," Finn said warily. "I'm starting to recognize that expression. What do you want from me, Doctor Chambers?"

"It's easy."

"What is it?"

"Simple," Lauren said with a smile. "Tell me what the 'T' stands for."

"What?"

"Finnegan T. Gallagher. What's the 'T' for?"

Finn grinned. "Forget it. I'm not telling."

"For a wedding present? Please?"

"No way. Think of something else."

"What is this? A state secret? What's your middle name?"

"I never tell anyone."

"Not even your wife?! Honestly, Finn, I'll go call your mother right this minute, if you—"

"All right, all right," he said, grabbing her back into the bed. "But you have to promise not to give the name to any of our kids."

"All right, all right, but I'm dying to know. What is it?"

He took a breath.

"Theobald? Thurston? Thaddeus?"

"No."

"Ted? Tom?"

"No. You'll never guess."

"What is it?"

Finn shut his eyes. "Tiffany."

"Tiffany?" Lauren hooted. "Tiffany!"

"Finnegan Tiffany Gallagher. The name's over a hundred years old."

"Tiffany! I love it! What a great name for a daughter!"

"Lauren!"

Giggling, she fell into his arms and rolled onto the bedclothes with him. He was perfect. A silly name and a sensitive, sometimes silly disposition. He was a gentle man, a boyish, wonderful, deeply caring man who looked at life the way Lauren decided everyone should, and he deserved the kindest treatment in return. In his arms, she made a vow. She smiled and said, "I love you, Finn. For always. You're special and you'll be special to me forever."

WONDERFUL ROMANCE NEWS!

Do you know about the exciting SECOND CHANCE AT LOVE/TO HAVE AND TO HOLD newsletter? Are you on our *free* mailing list? If reading all about your favorite authors, getting sneak previews of their latest releases, and being filled in on all the latest happenings and events in the romance world sound good to you, then you'll love our SECOND CHANCE AT LOVE and TO HAVE AND TO HOLD Romance News.

If you'd like to be added to our mailing list, just fill out the coupon below and send it in...and we'll send you your *free* newsletter every three months—hot off the press.

☐ *Yes, I would like to receive your free SECOND CHANCE AT LOVE/TO HAVE AND TO HOLD newsletter.*

Name _____

Address _____

City _____ **State/Zip** _____

Please return this coupon to:

Berkley Publishing
200 Madison Avenue, New York, New York 10016
Att: Rebecca Kaufman

HERE'S WHAT READERS ARE SAYING ABOUT

Second Chance at Love®

"I think your books are great. I love to read them, as does my family."
— _P. C., Milford, MA_*

"Your books are some of the best romances I've read."
— _M. B., Zeeland, MI_*

"SECOND CHANCE AT LOVE is my favorite line of romance novels."
— _L. B., Springfield, VA_*

"I think SECOND CHANCE AT LOVE books are terrific. I married my 'Second Chance' over 15 years ago. I truly believe love is lovelier the second time around!"
— _P. P., Houston, TX_*

"I enjoy your books tremendously."
— _I. S., Bayonne, NJ_*

"I love your books and read them all the time. Keep them coming—they're just great."
— _G. L., Brookfield, CT_*

"SECOND CHANCE AT LOVE books are definitely the best!"
— _D. P., Wabash, IN_*

*Name and address available upon request

Second Chance at Love®

All of the above titles are $1.95
Prices may be slightly higher in Canada.
